KILLERBOWL

KILLERBOWL

GARY K. WOLF

DOUBLEDAY & COMPANY, INC.

GARDEN CITY, NEW YORK

1975

All of the characters in this book are fictitious, and any resemblance to actual persons, living or dead, is purely coincidental.

Library of Congress Cataloging in Publication Data

Wolf, Gary K
  Killerbowl.

  I. Title.
PZ4.W8533Ki [PS3573.O483]   813′.5′4
ISBN 0-385-04738-X
Library of Congress Catalog Card Number 75-2857

To my mother and father.
For their sacrifices, their guidance, and their love.

SUPERBOWL XXI, THE DAY BEFORE

Friday, December 31, 2010, 7:55 P.M.

Sitting on the floor next to a practice bag full of footballs, T.K. takes one last riff through his play book, making some inconsequential notations in the margins as he goes.

For what must be the hundredth time in the past hour, he pulls out and studies his Boston street map, paying particular attention to the area bordered by Cambridge and Mt. Vernon Streets on the north and south, Bowdoin and Charles to the east and west.

Coach Carrerra enters the locker room and wordlessly hands him the latest weather forecast. Not too different from the weather of the last few days, bitter and bone-chillingly cold. The temperatures will range from fourteen above zero at the start of the game to thirty degrees at the game's midpoint, to a frigid five above when the game concludes tomorrow midnight. The chance of snowfall has declined from 50 to 30 per cent, but there'll still be great quantities of it on the street left over from last week's tumultuous storm.

The trainer calls T.K.'s name.

The familiar paraphernalia is all laid out, the tape, the scissors, the Band-Aids, the gauze. T.K. hops up on the training table, and the trainer sets to work. He applies flexible penetration-resistant aluminum tape along T.K.'s major arteries, up and down both sides of his neck, around both his wrists, around his elbows and around his thighs from groin to knee. He wraps conventional surgical tape around T.K.'s ankles and knees. He changes the dressing on T.K.'s injured left shoulder.

T.K. climbs off the table, flexes his wrists, elbows and thighs and rotates his neck and ankles to work the tape into his skin's natural creases.

Satisfied with the trainer's work, he goes to his locker, opens it, and begins the laborious process of suiting up.

First comes his aluminum groin cup—the infamous iron horse—and his elastic supporter.

To help fend off the cold, he slips on a set of ventilated thermal underwear.

Next, he straps on his kidney protectors, a series of narrow plastic slats lying vertically across the curvature of his back.

His slatted leggins, flexible resin ribbing covered with a half-inch of absorbent rubber, go on in two sections, one for his calf, one for his thigh. The two portions join together in an alloy hinge at the knee. Narrow-mesh metal mailing snaps into place over them.

Arm guards, thinner than his leggins but constructed and worn in exactly the same way, go on next.

Chest and back plates, also made of flexible resin, clamshell into place over his neck. The plates are supported by spring-mounted, energy-absorbing plastic braces contour fitted to his body. The braces neatly straddle the slats of his kidney protectors. The undersides of his chest and back plates are lined with a high-impact, penetration-resistant alloy.

Fiberglas-backed foam rubber shoulder and hip pads, a mail covering over his lower abdomen and groin, and a foam rubber cushion across the back of his neck round out his body-protective equipment.

He hooks on his garter belt, pulls on a knee-high pair of stockings, and fastens them up. He unrolls his snug blue uniform pants on over leggins, stockings, garter and pads. Because his team has been designated Visitor, he dons his blue and gold "away" jersey. He sticks his hand into the oblong pocket, the gut pocket, sewn into his jersey just over his stomach, to make certain it's fully open and empty. On long runs, the football will go in here leaving T.K. with both hands free to defend himself.

His shoes are high-topped and metal lined with rubber soles.

He has them equipped with deep suction cups for better footing on ice. Cleats of any type are expressly forbidden. He threads new laces into his shoes, tightens them up, then buckles a nylon strip over them to prevent their being cut during the game.

He double-checks the pressure on the inflatable bags in his honeycombed resin helmet. He also assures that there are no leaks in the ring of encased jelly that circumvents the helmet's base and affords a measure of extra comfort to his jaw and the back of his neck.

His polarized Plexiglas face mask, self-adjusting to give him correct glare protection under any degree of illumination, edges flawlessly into place in the frontal grooves incised around the facial opening of his helmet.

He slips his long knife into its sheath, and clips on his bola.

Lastly, he pulls on a pair of thin, resin-mesh gloves, the fingers and palms of which are open for better ball control.

He checks himself out in the locker room mirror, paying special attention to the way his uniform covers him in his most vulnerable areas, his hands, neck, the back of his knees, his inner elbows, and his inner groin, all sections of his body which, for one reason or another, can't be adequately protected. Turning his back to the mirror, he sees a gold ЄІ on his jersey and above it the gold letters ИИAM, his number and name, wrinkle-free and totally legible, the final item on his checklist.

Fully dressed and ready, he sits down on a bench, closes his eyes, and starts psyching himself up for the game.

It's 10 P.M. He has two hours before it starts.

Friday, January 1, 2010

"Let me try and summarize this heart-stopping situation for you, football fans," enunciates Timothy Enge, the renowned Voice of Football, facing the camera. "We have two minutes left on the clock. The San Francisco Prospectors trail the New England Minutemen 116 to 121. The Prospectors have the ball with 225 yards to go for a touchdown. They must score to win, and they're going to have an extremely hard time doing it. The Minutemen's defense, which has been murderous all day, has toughened up even more in these final minutes. Nothing is getting through." He loosens his tie and unsnaps his tunic, a gesture which, to his millions of viewers, each and every one thoroughly familiar with his compulsively fastidious nature, goes farther than anything he can say to convey the degree of pressure in the air. "But the Prospectors play the ever threatening brand of football that could still pull this game out of the fire. Twice this season alone, they've been down by one touchdown late in a game, and T.K. Mann has brought them back to win both times. The question is, can he make it three?" Enge turns from the camera. "Let's get down on the street and find out."

As the opposing teams line up on Van Ness, an estimated 250 million Americans watching at home collectively hold their breath.

T.K. Mann takes the snap, fakes a hand-off and drops back between two overflowing garbage cans to pass.

The line holds. He has all the time in the world.

But nobody opens up.

T.K. breaks a tackle, almost falling when his tackler stubbornly clings to him long enough to open a fleshy knife wound in his left knee, and cuts behind a light pole looking for his receiver.

The clock runs out, making this the last play of the game.

Still, nobody opens up.

T.K. reverses direction, scrambling for time.

At last! Wide receiver Fred Gradington shakes his man and breaks from the sidewalk into the street. There's nothing between him and the bay but 200 yards of wide open space.

T.K. cocks his arm.

Bumbo Johnson, All-Pro linebacker, six-eleven, two eighty-four, plunges through into the backfield and leaps.

T.K. lets go with the long bomb.

Bumbo Johnson tags T.K. with a powerful blow to the helmet. Stunned, T.K. goes down. Bumbo falls on him, knees first, and proceeds to give his kidneys a methodical working over with a short-handled club.

All alone out there in mid-street, Fred Gradington comes in under the ball for an easy grab.

As one, America jumps screaming to its feet.

Gradington, playing his first season, lifts his whole head skyward, instead of only his eyes as a more seasoned pro would have done, and reaches for the ball.

The Minutemen's hidden safety, crouching on the fifteenth floor of the Fontana West apartments, puts cross hairs on Gradington's Adam's apple, now ever so slightly exposed just below the bottom of his bulletproof helmet and mask, just above the top of his body armor, and squeezes the trigger.

Gradington and the football hit the street at almost the exact same instant.

A gunshot echoes through the street.

T.K. Mann loses consciousness.

Superbowl XX is over.

Saturday, January 2, 2010

"Marda," screams the man of the house, near to collapse from excitement. "Did you see that finish?"

His wife shambles forth from the kitchen, a bowl of pretzels in one hand, a half-empty beer in the other. "Yeah, Dreddie, I saw it out on the portable. It sure was thrilling."

"I should hope to tell you. Thrilling ain't even the word." He cocks his head pleadingly. "Want to watch it again?"

Creases turn her brow into a meaty washboard. "Gee, I dunno, Dreddie. Can we afford it? I mean, we're way over our base replay time, already. It's all extra for the rest of the month."

"So we go into hock a little. So what? I mean, my God, Marda, how often do you see a finish like that?"

"Well, I suppose we could both work some overtime. Maybe cut down on snacks or . . ."

Content to let Marda worry about the economics of it, Dreddie is already at the set. He adjusts a dial, punches a code into a matrix of buttons, pushes the replay switch, joins Marda on the sofa, and helps himself to a drink of her beer.

The set winks to life, spews out an animated deodorant commercial (this at no charge) and fades in Dreddie's rerun selection.

Their eyes wide, their mouths full of pretzels, living color splashing death on their faces, Dreddie and Marda watch once again the last five minutes of Fred Gradington's life.

Saturday, January 2, 2010

T.K. collapses onto a bench in front of his locker, involuntarily jerks halfway back up in an all-over spasm of pain, then lowers himself, slowly this time, consciously forcing his body to ignore the exploding nerve endings that would send him screaming back into space. Jesus but that Johnson can handle a short club. T.K. rubs his kidneys, especially sore from Johnson's repeated thrashings, and his chest, which burns in parallel lines where the braces for his body armor have been shoved, time and again today, up against his ribs.

He has the whole locker room, a large mobile trailer, at least temporarily to himself. His teammates are still out on the street telling Timothy Enge and his viewers how next year they're going to come back, come back and win XXI. The breaks went against us, they were saying when he left them. We'll get the breaks back next year. Sure they will. T.K.'s heard the same story with minor variations a million times before. Bad breaks. The loser's lament.

T.K. isn't out there with them joining in on the chorus because he doesn't have the stomach for that kind of self-absolving delusion. T.K.'s a realist. He knows the Prospectors didn't lose that game because of bad breaks. They lost because Harv

Matision, the Minutemen's rookie quarterback, faked T.K. Mann right out of his iron horse. The apartment house. How obvious could Matision have been? Putting his hidden safety in the God-damned apartment house. It was so obvious. A clear shot in any direction. T.K. should have guessed it at once. Then he would have thrown that last pass to Gradington's right side instead of to his left. That way, when Gradington got excited, as T.K. should have realized he would, and lifted his head, the kid would have had his back to the apartment house instead. His neck would have been covered and the best the hidden safety could have hoped for would have been a lucky shot to the inside of Gradington's knee, to the quarter-inch opening where thigh and calf ribbing come together.

T.K. shifts around in his seat, trying to find a position that will relieve the pain in a majority of his injured parts. The fact that he can't resurrects the nagging realization that's been festering within him for so long now. He's getting old. Thirty-four. What the newscaster on the six o'clock sports roundup refers to as an aging quarterback. It's probably the worst kept secret in the league that the Prospectors' head office has been scouting around for months for some new quarterback, some new *young* quarterback to replace him. After that mediocre showing he put up against Matision today, they're undoubtedly looking even harder.

Christ, how he wished it didn't matter. How he wished he could just say screw 'em and retire. Live a Sunday without pain.

But the plain and simple truth is, he can't afford to. Always fast with a dollar, T.K. Mann is broke. Where did it all go? Twelve years' worth of six-figure salaries, that much again in endorsement money? Simple. It went to buy gasoline for his car, pay the rent on his parents' farmhouse and on his fancy penthouse apartment on Russian Hill, and, more often than not, it went to buy him and some impressionable young lady an honest-to-God real meat dinner at Ernie's.

While he hasn't as yet undertaken any sweeping economy measures, nowadays he does live week to week, totally reliant on his football paycheck to meet his expenses. The sweet promotional deals that used to fall into his lap every time he laid a touchdown pass into a teammate's waiting arms have all but petered out as the sporting goods companies, the department stores, the bicycle firms search out someone that the youth of America can more easily identify with, someone strong, victorious and young.

Unfortunately, there's no such thing as a pension fund in the Street Football League. Players get a fat salary and a big, paid-up life insurance policy, instead. Most guys, T.K. in his younger days included, figure it to be a lot more realistic deal that way.

So T.K. plays football, and will keep playing football until the head office throws him out on his ass, or some linebacker fuses his kidneys to the street.

The exhaustion that T.K. has ignored for the past twenty-four hours finally overcomes him and drags him down into sleep, but even here he gets no relief. Like a nightmarish spike, the pain punches holes in his dreams.

SUPERBOWL XXI, THE DAY BEFORE

Friday, December 31, 2010, 10:30 P.M.

Mentally, he's as ready as he'll ever be, his desire sharpened to a killing edge, his concentration honed to a pinpoint, his pain shoved far to the back of his mind. But most of T.K.'s teammates are still undergoing the strange rituals men sustain to prepare themselves to face death.

Varnie Pfleg, a tackle/lineman, sits in perfect silence on the floor off in a corner, his hands cupping his face, his legs spread open in a V in front of him. From time to time, he slides his hands open and peers down between his thighs. There lies a full-color hologram of his wife and three children.

Orval Frazier, the fullback/middle linebacker, stands with his helmet on, his back to the locker room's forward bulkhead, the one separating the dressing area from the trainer's room.

With metronomic regularity, he lets his head drop forward, then, in a snapping motion, slams it full force backwards into the wall. Frazier has been All-Pro for the past four seasons. He's generally considered to be the toughest man in football.

Harland Minick, center/lineman, Lester Brye, guard/lineman, and Hellinger Clausen, halfback/deep safety, sit in a circle in the middle of the floor. All of them have rosary beads. Minick, an ex-altar boy, leads them in prayer.

Ken Dedemus, a guard/lineman, never suits up until minutes before the team goes out onto the street for warm-ups. He spends his pre-game hours in the locker room shower letting the water run across his shoulders, down his back and chest. Every half hour or so, he masturbates.

The most unflappable man on the team, Lammy Howe, a halfback/deep safety, takes a nap, spread out under the trainer's table. His snores echo loudly throughout the room.

Ros DeGeller and Mike Michalski, the ends, slap each other's shoulder pads and trade light combinations of punches, mostly uppercuts and jabs.

Kneeling in a corner, Buddy Healy, a tackle/lineman, throws up into a gray plastic bucket. Zack Rauscher, the mediman, holds him by the shoulders, giving him what little comfort he can.

Gus D'Armato, the hidden safety, dry fires his rifle, drawing in on a target pasted to his locker door, slowly squeezing his trigger, SNAP.

There are two large bowls set out, one on the trainer's table, one on a bench in the dressing room. Both contain a smorgasbord assortment of pills, brand name uppers donated by leading pharmaceutical companies in return for free endorsements. Most players sort through on their way by, pluck out and ingest a few of their favorites. T.K., in line with his long-held belief that a reliance on chemicals for extra endurance shortens long-term playing life, abstains, although he doesn't feel the slightest bit of disdain for those who don't. So long as his teammates perform at par on the street, he couldn't care less what they do off it.

Coach Carrerra enters the locker room and calls for attention. A swarm of giant man-slaying moths drawn to the flame of inspiration, his players step forward and surround him.

"I'm not going to give you any long sermon," he says. "We all know what we're here for, we all know what we have to do." He reaches into his handbag and pulls out a newspaper clipping. "Before you go out there, I do want to read you something, though. This is from yesterday's *Chronicle*. I thought you might like to hear what Harv Matision has to say about Superbowl XXI. 'This Superbowl stuff is getting to be kind of old hat to me,' he says. 'I mean, it gets kind of repetitious. Every New Year's Day, regular as clockwork, I kick hell out of the Prospectors. I wouldn't complain if it was at least good exercise but, hell, I'd get more of a workout by staying home and getting laid, although I guess playing the Prospectors is almost the same thing. Either way, I wind up giving a bunch of pussies a good fucking over.'"

Carrerra wads the sheet up and tosses it on the floor. "After something like that, do I have to get you up? Do I have to give you a reason to go out and win this game? Look up there." He points to a faded XXI written in chalk on the locker room blackboard. "That's where we've been going all year, and now we're here. Why? Because we're the best damn team in the league. We're winners. And we're gonna show 'em we're winners. Matision, the Minutemen, and the whole God-damned world. Now, let's go out there and play football."

Orval Frazier hits the locker room door. "Fucking aye," he screams, and he's out on the street. The rest of the team follows after.

T.K. hangs back. From here on, Carrerra is little different from millions of other Americans. He'll watch the game on television just like everybody else, nothing less, nor more, than an observer to its self-ordained ebb and flow. He's performed his function, done his duty. He's given his men everything he thinks they need to win. It's too late now to take part of it back or add more. Sure, he'll see them at the quarter time-outs, but in less than an hour he can't undo much of what will have gone on in the five and a half hours before. For the most part, when his last man takes to the street to start the game, he enters a state of limbo, powerless to aid in victory, a foremost object of blame in defeat.

"Any final instructions?" T.K. asks as if there could really be any that mattered.

Carrerra stares balefully up into T.K.'s eyes. He has genuinely solicitous emotion in his voice when he speaks. "Just go out and win the son of a bitch, T.K., just you go out on that street and you win."

T.K. nods, and trots out after his team.

Saturday, February 20, 2010

"Hey, T.K." Pressing into service the same swivel-hipped motion that has made him the league's leading ground gainer for the past two seasons, Ripper Henry, fullback/deep safety with the Chicago Hawks, picks his way through the clubhouse crowd. T.K. raises his arm, hand open and extended, in a greeting which Ripper returns. "How's the knees?" Ripper asks.

It's always like that when two pros meet, almost a formalized ritual. First the open-handed gesture, then an inquiry after the levels of pain, the latter being the universal professional concern that transcends the nagging realization there will undoubtedly come a Sunday when one of these men might be forced to kill the other.

"They've got so many metal staples in them, they clang when I bump them together. Damn glad I'm not knock-kneed. How's your shoulder? I was watching the play-off on TV when you took that point-blank shot." Despite Ripper's having a tremendous Sunday, rushing for nearly 400 yards, the Hawks lost their division play-off and their shot at the Superbowl to Matision and the Minutemen.

His hand fisted, Ripper swings his arm in a wide circle, stopping about a quarter of the way around. "Stiff, right there." He brings his other hand up, and pantomimes a golf swing.

"But I got a hundred-dollar bill says I whip the pants off you, today."

The two are participating in the Temple Beth Al Pro-Am Golf Tournament, an annual affair held in Atlanta during the ten-week break football players are given between season's end and the start of spring training.

T.K. nods to acknowledge the bet. "How about we go lubricate our aching joints until it's time." He dips his head in the direction of the bar, completely surrounded by athletes, all waiting for their turn to tee off.

"Best play you've called all year." Ripper angles his way effortlessly into the solid wall of thirsty muscle.

T.K. starts after him, when a hand gently touches his bicep. "You're T.K. Mann." A statement, not a question, spoken in a smoky, feminine voice that rises like a sigh through the heavy rumbles of drinking men.

He turns. She's tall, five-eleven, maybe, only three inches shorter than he is. He likes tall girls, so much so that before checking her out any further, he sneaks a quick look at her feet to see how much of her stature comes from platform heels. None of it, as it turns out. She's wearing flats. Impressed, he evaluates the rest of her. If she's a team follower, she's a cut above any T.K. has ever run across. There's a sophisticated patina to her. Her hair is long, sandy brown, piled demurely up over her head in tiny braids. She doesn't wear makeup, but then, she doesn't seem to need it. Her skin has a nice, healthy sheen to it, blending well with her naturally dark lips. Her slacks, double-breasted coat, patterned shirt and matching tie are mannish, what all women are sporting this season, but with her long lines and trim figure she's one of the few girls who, in T.K.'s opinion, manage to bring a degree of femininity to the fashion.

"Mr. Mann, my brother is quite a fan of yours. Do you suppose . . . ?" Tenuously, she offers him a cocktail napkin and a pen. "It would mean an awfully lot to him."

"Glad to. And please call me T.K." He takes the napkin and pen. "Miss . . . ?"

"Lauffler. Sarah."

"What's your brother's name, Sarah?"

"Zachary."

"O.K. How's this?" He autographs the napkin, personalizing it to Zachary, and hands it back.

She reads it and smiles, her lips moist and slightly parted. "He'll be tickled to death."

"So will I if you'll join me for a drink."

Again, she smiles. "All right. An eagle's wing, perhaps."

T.K. calls out to Ripper, who has just secured the services of a bartender. "Rip, how 'bout bringing back a scotch over ice and an eagle's wing, will you?"

Ripper sees the girl, and dips his head to acknowledge the order.

T.K. guides Sarah to the rear of the bar, where the noise level isn't quite as overpowering. "Are you here with somebody?" he asks.

"No, just an interested observer." From out of her shoulder bag, she pulls a small, pastel-colored pipe of the straight-stemmed, curved-bowl variety currently in vogue among women, and tamps it full of a sweetish tobacco. "I'm a free-lance writer doing an article on Temple Beth Al. I came here to the tournament because I thought I might be able to pick up some colorful sidelights. I'm afraid I'm not having much success, though," she confesses. "Everything I know about athletics I learned last night by skimming this." She shows him a paperback overview of professional sports authored by a top national sportswriter. "I'm completely out of my element, here."

Ripper arrives with their drinks, but almost immediately the loudspeaker announces him as being in the next foursome to tee off. He downs his drink and heads for the door. A small man, barely five-three, maybe 110 pounds, hustles after him. "Ripper," the man shouts out. "Wait up. They got us in the same foursome."

"Don't tell me. Some pro's using you for a putter," Ripper jokes, giving the man as much of the open-handed, arm-raised

greeting as the closely packed crowd allows. The two head for
the door together.

"My goodness," Sarah says, watching them go, "the man
who came up to Ripper. He's so tiny. Does he play a sport?"

"That's Dale Slade. He plays football for the Fort Worth
Devils."

Her lips purse and her eyes widen in mild surprise. "Admit-
tedly, I'm not very familiar with athletics"—she puffs rapidly on
her pipe, her cloying tobacco drawing unappreciative stares
from some of the athletes around her—"but he seems awfully
small to be a football player."

T.K. shakes his head. "Not at all. Actually, he's probably the
most important man on the team, even though he never takes
part in the plays. He's the Devils' mediman. He gives on-street
medical aid to injured players."

She removes the pipe from her mouth and holds it by the
bowl, twisting tiny corkscrews in the air with the stem. "Surely
if a player's injured badly enough to require medical help, he's
taken off the street. Brought to a hospital."

Taking pity on her for her naïveté, T.K. patiently explains
the most basic rule of football. "There are no substitutions in a
football game. The players who start a game are required to
stay in until they finish it, either that or until the game finishes
them. Nobody comes out, not for anything, injuries included."

"That's unbelievable. Football games last a whole day. So a
man who's incapacitated early on in the game can't be taken off
the street until it's over?"

"No, it's not quite that harsh. An injured man can be removed during one of the quarter time-outs. That means the
longest a wounded man would ever have to stay on the street is
five and a half hours."

"My God. What if he dies?"

"That's what the mediman tries to prevent. He puts a big red
cross on an injured player. That makes it illegal for the opposition to attack him. It also makes it illegal for the injured man to
take part in a play. When, and if, the mediman gets him

patched up, the red cross comes off, and he's back in the game."

"What if everybody on a team gets red-crossed?"

"The other team wins, regardless of the score. It's kind of football's version of the knockout. But it rarely happens. We generally don't lose more than a few men a game. First of all, our uniform gives us a good deal of protection. And pro football players are fanatical when it comes to building up their endurance, stamina and conditioning. That's why you're getting so many unkind stares right now."

She glances about, noticing it for the first time.

He points to her pipe. "The smoke. It's a professional taboo. Cuts the wind. The vast majority of players avoid it like the plague."

"Oh, I'm terribly sorry. I didn't know." Self-consciously, she taps out her pipe.

"Don't worry about it. I've always considered it rather hypocritical. The players who are most vehement about not smoking are usually the same ones who shoot themselves full of every drug in the book to keep going during a game."

"Do you do that?"

"No. I feel that kind of stuff cuts down your long-term efficiency, not to mention your life-span. I play it straight. I get plenty of rest the day before a game. Maybe I take a nap between quarters."

She tilts her head to one side, trying in vain to conceal her perplexed curiosity. "Forgive me if I'm encroaching on some sensitive topic, but from everything you've just told me, I get the distinct impression that the secret to being a successful football player is having the ability to injure others without being injured in return. To me, that indicates a terribly casual regard for human life. Don't you find it disturbing to play such a game?"

"I'm sure some players do. I never have, though. Hell, I didn't make up the rules. I just abide by them. Killing is part of football. If you can't accept that, you shouldn't be playing."

"You've killed other players, then?"

"Of course. Just as they would have killed me had they gotten the chance."

"It all sounds so callous."

"Believe me, it's not. It's the professional attitude. Sure I hate to see good men get hurt. But football players get paid big money to take physical risks, to die, if their luck goes bad, for the enjoyment of the fans. I try hard to protect my players, as hard as any quarterback in the league. My lost player ratio, the LPR you'll hear people talking about if you follow the game, is only one point something, good for maybe second from the bottom in the league. So you know what that gets me? Sportswriters criticize my game for being colorless. Even my own head office sometimes chews me out for being too conservative. You'd think they'd be happy that I keep their personnel losses down, keep them from having to go out after a game and recruit new players. But it's not that way at all. The head office has to please the fans to turn a profit. The fans pay to see blood. I'm supposed to see that they do. It's as simple as that. Take the quarterback I faced in the Superbowl. Harv Matision. He plays football like a wounded animal, kill-or-be-killed. Yet that's what makes for an exciting ball game, so the fans idolize him."

"This LPR you mentioned. What's Matision's?"

"Four even. Highest in the league. He loses a lot of his men."

"I also win a lot of games," comes a deep-throated growl from behind them. They both turn to face Harv Matision. His spread-legged posture, hands on hips, displays to best advantage his deep chest, long legs, his power. His eyes are incendiary, his mouth twisted and mocking. Symbolically, he doesn't give T.K. the open-handed greeting. "Isn't that right, old man?" He puts callous arrogance into it, the way a cocky youngster might address an elderly cripple.

T.K. has slim regard for Matision on the field, absolutely none off. "This is kind of a private conversation, Matision. Butt out."

"Sure, old man. Just wanted to come over and pay my respects to the league's second best quarterback." He fairly oozes conceit. "See you outside. I think they're about ready to call our foursome."

"*Our* foursome?"

"Yeah. They've got us playing together, me teamed with Murado, you with Ibsem. The matchmakers thought it would be an interesting draw. Kind of an eighteen-hole replay of the Superbowl. Clever, huh?"

"More diabolical, I'd say," T.K. responds.

Matision winks at Sarah. "You see, there are still a few assholes out there saying T.K. Mann's better than I am, and it's up to me to convince 'em otherwise. Your boyfriend, here, he knows I can do it, too. He knows I will do it. He knows that somehow, somewhere, I'm gonna kill him."

"And he's the president of my fan club," T.K. says lightly. "You should hear a few of the guys who hate me."

"You can't laugh me off your back, old man," rasps Matision. "Sooner or later, I'm gonna spread your guts all over a sidewalk." Drawing his index finger across the general area of T.K.'s midsection, he wheels, and swaggers off into the crowd.

"He can't be serious," gasps Sarah, her eyes two shocked round disks.

"He is. Deadly serious. He's made no secret of it for quite some time."

"But why?"

"Because he thinks he's better than I am."

"Is he?"

T.K. doesn't answer right away. When he does, his words are low, barely audible. "Well, he's younger, that's for sure."

Before Sarah can follow up with another question, the loudspeaker blares out the names of Murado, Ibsem, Matision and Mann, asking them to report to the first tee.

T.K. tosses down his drink. "Coming?"

"No, I don't feel up to hassling the crowd. I think I'll watch it in here on TV."

"O.K. Look, I usually get into Atlanta a couple of times during the season. Can I see you next time? For dinner, maybe?"

"I'd like that. Buzz me up. I'm in the book. And good luck with your match."

"Thanks. I'll be in touch." T.K. picks up his clubs at the door, and goes out.

As soon as he's gone, Sarah reaches inside her shoulder bag and turns off her tape recorder. She pops out the thumbnail-sized cassette, tosses it up and down several times in her palm as if weighing the import of the words it contains, and drops it into a side pocket.

She walks outside and removes her rented bicycle from its locked parking rack. She mounts and pedals off, tossing her sports book and T.K.'s autographed napkin into the first garbage pail she rides by.

Saturday, February 20, 2010

The jazz band barely drowns out the sound of the TV over the bar. ". . . almost came to blows," says the sportscaster, showing a hole-by-hole replay of the bitter golfing battle waged that day between T.K. and Matision. "Harv Matision went on to win both that personal contest, and, together with his partner, Jose Murado, the tournament itself. To this newsman, it was a symbolic victory. Coming as it does on top of Matision's stunning Superbowl performance, it firmly solidifies his position as the top athlete in the nation, the man to beat not only in football, but in total ability and guts, as well."

T.K. sits in with the band, playing drums, the staccato rhythms of cymbal and snare covering up not only the sportscaster's commentary, but also the bitter drone of defeat that still echoes inside his brain.

No doubt about it, this just hasn't been his day.

After the tournament, he'd tried to buzz Sarah Lauffler, but the information operator told him there was no such person listed either in Atlanta or in any town within a twelve-mile radius. So, twice defeated, he came here, fully intending to drink himself into painless oblivion.

chooses humiliation over bloodletting. In
ts the seat out of Matision's leather pants,
hind.

fe into the floor and breaks it.

cocktail waitress over. "Honey, get the
of milk and a clean set of diapers, will you?"
red-dollar bill—Ripper Henry's an even worse
.—down the front of her dress. "And keep the

ks into the cool night air, Matision calls out be-
ann, you son of a bitch. I'll get you for this. I'll get
me, and I'll fix you for keeps."

what I like about this sport," whispers T.K. under his
ou make such wonderful friends." He hops into a
or the trip back to his hotel.

PERBOWL XXI, THE DAY BEFORE

Friday, December 31, 2010, 11:00 P.M.

e Prospectors assemble at the intersection of Pinckney and
edar. T.K. lines them up in two rows, six men in one, five in
he other (since the mediman doesn't carry the ball or engage
in contact, he's exempted), and puts them through their warm-
ups. He leads off with jumping jacks, squat presses and roll-
overs to loosen legs, bodies and arms. Then he launches into the
tough stuff, the one-on-ones, the head-jerkers, the roustabouts.

An icy wind swirls in out of the northeast. It takes the top
layer of snow and stitches it into a white, all-enveloping curtain. The streetlights, on all throughout the playing area, cast a
harsh phosphorescence that gives at least major streets a sem-
blance of daylight. The buildings, though, and the vacant lots
and the back alleys are as dark as a bottomless hole, and, during a game, oftentimes just as deadly to step into.

The section of Boston they're playing in was once the habitat
of Brahmins and the socially elite. Now it's a hodgepodge of

The band finish‑
way Baffle," w‑
appears. H
leather
abo‑
him
derag‑

"Set
myself a
everybody
Then he see
Mann. Since you
ting down." He t
shout, now, to make
in the bar. "How ab
drummer?" He rocks ba

Silently, T.K. puts aside
for him, under perfect, and a
spreads his arms in a circle abo
feet around. T.K. steps inside it.

"How do you want it?" T.K. ask
"Any way you think you can hand
swers, at the same time swinging his ri
present a smaller target. His right arm
knife.

It's over so quickly, it's hard to believe the
two of the country's leading masters in the art o
combat.

T.K. slides sideways, ducking the knife, comes i
bends back Matision's elbow. As Matision's arm stiff
rams his knee into Matision's kidney, once, twice, three
and pushes him, sagging, headfirst into the bar. T.K. set
heel to Matision's right hand, and grinds it around until
knife falls free. Then he kicks Matision twice in the ribs.

Gasping for breath, Matision doubles over. T.K. stoops, picks
up the knife, and grabs Matision by the seat of the pants. He
puts the knife point to Matision's rear end. The crowd gasps in

20
expectation, but T.K.
four neat slices, he c
exposing his bare b
T.K. jams the kn
He calls the
youngster a glass
He stuffs a hund
golfer than T.K.
change."
As T.K. wa
hind him. "N
you in a ga
"That's
breath. "
pedicab

SU
Th
C
t

middle-class row houses, light industry and shabby shopping centers. There are several tall modern office buildings rising up out of the midst of it all like great glass and chrome tombstones marking the passage of better, more refined days beneath. The area also includes the Institute of Contemporary Art and portions of Suffolk University, an inclusion that makes the players quite happy. The long, winding corridors of cultural institutions or of academia afford many places for a truly determined individual to hide out, often for long stretches of time. Louisburg Square is also within the game's boundaries. The square is an historic landmark, a fine collection of old town houses and cobblestone streets, sadly run down, but still displaying a layer of charm and grace beneath a surface covering of grime and neglect.

The streets are eerily quiet. T.K.'s calisthenic commands echo off empty buildings, careen down deserted streets, float with the wind, billow up with the snow. The Prospectors grunt in their labors, their feet making squishy sounds as the force of their exercises melts the snow beneath them. Once, there would have been spectators here to watch them, to cheer them on, but that was long ago, when the league first began. The spectators quickly proved to be a major hindrance to the game. Not only were they in great danger themselves, but they frequently spoiled the workings of a beautiful play by shouting out to a favored player the location of the man he pursued. Therefore, spectators are banned.

At approximately eleven-twenty, the referees come out wearing bright red and yellow striped coveralls, and glow-yellow caps. They carry large flashlights. Each one has a whistle and a portable amplifier permitting him to make himself heard over a three-square-block area. To communicate amongst themselves, they're equipped with belt-packed two-way transmitters, miniature ear-inserted receivers and throat mikes. They use the transmitters to co-ordinate reconvening the players at the end of each play, and also to receive details of the forthcoming play as broadcast over a specially guarded hush channel by the quarterback's referee, who sits in on the huddle.

There are thirteen referees, one for each player, paired by lottery the week prior to the game. At this moment, at the other end of the playing area, another thirteen referees are matching themselves up with their appropriate Minutemen. Since stealth is such a major factor in football, there are eight additional referees scattered around the playing area. If a play involves a planned deceptive run and hide, the ball carrier's regular referee will drop his coverage once the deception starts, and one or more of the eight unassigned referees will pick it up, but from a point of concealment. Naturally, if a deception is a spur-of-the-moment occurrence, the ball carrier's assigned referee will have no choice but to follow along.

A new squad of referees will replace this one at the beginning of the second quarter.

The cameramen trail out next. Here, also, one is assigned exclusively to each player. In addition, one cameraman covers each goalyard, and twelve roam about at will shooting provocative sidelights and overall play action. The cameramen are dressed in international orange coveralls. They wield fist-sized cameras with dyno-rotating lens turrets, each lens being easily as big as the camera itself. They wear a power pack on their back, its single pencil-thick cable attached to an automatic inertial take-up and play-out reel so they always have just as much slack as they need, no more. Their light-bulb-shaped helmets are jam-packed with the microwave gear necessary for sending out their TV signals and receiving instructions from the control room. Their focusing goggles are etched with prismatic sights operated by imperceptible movements of their pupils. A cable runs from their goggles to their cameras, permitting them to focus their cameras on an object merely by looking at it. They have special infrared attachments for use at night.

A directional, rotating pickup mike, gyroscopically synchronized to always point in the same direction as their camera, is mounted to a swivel on top of their helmet. The control room monitors the quarterback's calls through these mikes and, after having done so, relays the cameramen their shooting instructions.

Like the referees, the cameramen will work only six hours out of the game's twenty-four. Also like the referees, they have colleagues stationed around the playing area to pick up the ball carrier on any deceptive maneuver.

One of the two co-head referees, both of whom will preside at the coin toss before taking up a position with the program co-ordinator in the television control room, brings over the two goalyard referees and the two scrimmage line referees, and introduces them to T.K.

T.K. instructs his players to run pass patterns. He then goes off with the co-head referee.

At Anderson and Pinckney streets, the other co-head referee meets them. He has Harv Matision with him. One of the co-head referees says, "Harv Matision, Captain of the New England Minutemen, meet T.K. Mann, Captain of the San Francisco Prospectors."

T.K. extends his hand. Matision ignores it. "Flip the fucking coin and let's play ball." He sneers.

"Mr. Mann," the referee says, "as visiting team, please call heads or tails while the coin is in the air." He throws the coin spinning skyward.

"Heads."

Three cameramen, T.K.'s, Matision's and one of the rovers, perch about a half block away, covering the toss by way of long-range, telephoto lenses. The cameramen never get too close to the players for several reasons. They don't get all tangled up in the action that way, an important consideration with forty-eight cameramen involved, and, probably of more importance to them personally, it keeps them out of the way of an accidental knife thrust or rifle shot.

The coin comes down tails.

"We'll receive," says Matision.

"We'll defend the west goal," says T.K. The playing area isn't exactly rectangular. The west end is slightly wider than the east. T.K.'s selection will give the Prospectors the east goal in the final quarter, a tactical advantage. Late in the game, when both teams are always dog tired and often shorthanded, it helps to have a small area surrounding your goalyard—it cuts down on your opponent's mobility. Conversely, a large area around your opponent's goalyard gives you more mobility of your own.

The referee, for the benefit of the people watching at home, conveys the results of the coin toss via exaggerated arm motions in the direction of Matision's cameraman.

"You may both return to your teams," he says.

One of the co-head referees accompanies T.K. back to where his teammates, still shagging passes, await.

At precisely 11:45 P.M., the co-head referee again approaches T.K. "Your hidden safety, please."

T.K. motions Gus D'Armato forward. D'Armato comes, clutching his rifle as if it's an integral part of his arm.

The referee extends his hand palm up. In it is a 7.62 millimeter rifle bullet. D'Armato takes it, and slips it into the breech of his rifle, a specially made, single-shot pro-model Remington with a 12 x 50 day/night-light scope mounted on it. It's a superbly accurate sniping weapon. Hidden safeties throughout the league are pretty evenly split between it and a similar model manufactured by Winchester. D'Armato actually prefers the Winchester, but his Remington TV commercials double his yearly income, and dictate his choice in the game.

Loaded and ready, his cameraman and referee tagging along behind, D'Armato trots down Pinckney, cuts right onto Louisburg Square and disappears. He'll follow the action from a distance, responding according to secret signals he and T.K. arranged between them before the game. T.K. will either have him hide out in a tall building if the situation warrants the expenditure of his bullet, or will signal him to try and stalk the ball carrier and attempt to knife him on the ground.

T.K. has a good deal of latitude in hidden safety positioning since the hidden safety (as well as the mediman, although for more altruistic purposes) is not required to be on side at the start of a play. Because of this uninhibited spatial freedom, the hidden safety (again like the mediman) isn't permitted to carry the football, something allowed every other member of the team, backs and linemen alike.

T.K. marshals his teammates, gives them a few last words of encouragement, joins them for a communal handshake, and leads them toward Myrtle Street, there to line up for the kickoff.

Monday, February 22, 2010

Pierce Spencer, president of the International Broadcasting Company, is nicely summarized by one word. Control. That's what he does best, that's what he most enjoys. Nothing in IBC escapes his domination. He selects camera angles, auditions actors, chooses costumes, rewrites scripts, everything. He influences every aspect of IBC programming, delegating as little of his authority as possible. Management experts, when confronted with his administrative possessiveness, have been known to throw up their clipboards in horror. It can't work, they decide, but their theories unravel around them, because it does, and well.

Spencer is seated at his desk, surrounded by the yardsticks of his success, the golden statuettes, the framed certificates, the upward-soaring graphs depicting advertising and replay revenues.

He tilts back in his oversized chair, an expensive orthopedically proper affair constructed out of authentic leather and genuine wood, and lights a cigar, a Cuban cigar. Only the best for Pierce Spencer. In everything. He eats real meat and salad once a day, every day. He lives in a posh suburban penthouse. Periodic visits to a European health spa keep his body smooth and hearty. Occasional trips to a plastic surgeon do the same for his face. Wealthy enough to afford the fuel, important enough to ignore tough environmental protection laws, he even owns and regularly uses the ultimate status symbol, a private, gasoline-powered automobile.

Assorted producers, directors and vice-presidents seated

around him squirm in rock-hard polychrome chairs. The chairs are purposefully uncomfortable. Pierce Spencer never lets his subordinates feel at ease in his presence.

This gathering, called an executive conference, is that in nomenclature only. It would be more properly termed a soliloquy, a monologue, possibly even a law-giving. At this meeting, Pierce Spencer will talk, everyone else will listen. Here, in this building, in this organization, in this hermetically sealed 200-story world, Pierce Spencer rules. Anyone questioning that rule, or that ruler, is dealt with, sometimes in very long-lasting ways. It's that simple.

The source of Pierce Spencer's authority, the power by which he governs, derives from a very simple gift. He has an almost mystical ability to gauge what the public wants, and to provide it. Years ago, amid a great deal of derision, he gambled on his instincts and secured exclusive long-term broadcasting rights to all SFL games. Today, his network runs little else, broadcasting games live on Sundays and rerunning highlights midway through the week. It's an astoundingly narrow range of programming, but it's remarkably successful. Street football, by any standard, is easily the most popular spectator sport of all time. It's made IBC a household fixture all across the country—most families have two sets, one of which is kept permanently tuned to the network—and it's made Pierce Spencer into a very rich and powerful man.

Spencer addresses his employees, using his cigar as a pointer to punctuate his remarks. "Last year, our street football coverage regularly attracted an eighty per cent share of audience." He slaps his hand to his desk, sending a fine shower of cigar ashes cascading to the floor. "This year, our audience share is going to improve. The approaching football season will be even more successful, even more profitable than last." He pauses to let the ramifications of his prediction sink in.

"It's going to be more successful, more profitable because we're going to increase the excitement potential of the games we cover, we're going to heighten the suspense, amplify the action. Our viewers want more killings, the sight of more blood.

So we're going to give it to them." He puffs out a massive cloud of blue-black smoke. "This year, we're going to double the number of football players under our direction. Moulay"—he points his cigar toward a middle-aged woman—"you take care of it. By the start of the season, I want there to be thirty-two players rigged up, one on every SFL team. That way, we're certain to have two of our players in every game we cover. Use our sports personality profiles to unearth likely candidates. When you feel you've found them, clear them with me. If I agree, you'll offer them the usual proposition. A hundred thousand dollars to let us implant the receiver, another fifty thousand for every man they kill during a game. Make sure they understand that we'll be relaying the ball carrier's position to them from the control room so they'll have more killing opportunities than their teammates. And don't neglect to tell them that we'll use the same technique, relayed information, to keep them out of trouble, and alive. I've found that to be the most effectively persuasive aspect of all. Any questions?"

The woman nods her head resolutely.

A balding, bespectacled man seated squarely in one corner of the room timidly pokes up his hand. "Sir," he says, "I have an objection I'd like to air." Spencer recognizes this major affront to prescriptive compliance by curling his lip and firmly shaking his cigar. But the man stands and begins to speak, anyway.

"Sir, I don't mean to be a naysayer, but I've done a great deal of factorial research into our involvement with the games, and I'm afraid if we expand our influence much further, we may reach a point of diminishing, even totally self-destructive returns." Now that he's started, he talks faster, as if to get it all said before Spencer's disapproving stare disintegrates him. "By keeping our operatives to a minimum, we've been able to maintain the discretion our activity demands. If we double the number of players we have in our service, we also double our risk of exposure. I'm afraid that sooner or later, one of our players, driven by morality or conscience, may betray our trust. In addition, there's always the possibility of blackmail—or if one of our players should ever be killed and undergo an autopsy, well, I needn't tell you how catastrophic the findings would turn out to be. I mean, a good case could be made for indicting us all as accessories to murder, not to mention the lesser, although certainly significant charge of interfering with interstate commerce. With the sixteen players we already have under our control, on the average we channel the outcomes of one half of all SFL games every season. I think that's enough. I see no reason to be greedy. I suggest, therefore, that we maintain our program at current levels, forsaking the added revenues, and the attendant risks it would take to broaden our operations." His courage, as well as his proposition, drained out of him, he drops to his chair.

His answer is quick in coming. "I don't agree with you, Deutsch," snarls Spencer. "And I doubt if anybody else does, either. Does anybody else?"

Naturally not. Pierce Spencer has very unsubtle methods for dealing with dissension.

"So, it's settled," Spencer says, "this season we buy ourselves thirty-two players, one on every team." And thus ends another IBC executive conference.

So You Want to Field a Football Team

For those of you out there who have always wanted to field your own professional street football team, this is the chapter where I tell you how to do it.

First, you start by robbing a bank.

In case you wonder why, here's a breakdown of what it costs to put the Prospectors out on the street.

Helmets and extra inflatable liners and jelly casings go for around $135 each. A lineman who does a lot of head blocking can go through six, maybe eight in a season. Plus, short clubs crack them open a lot, and we have to throw them away because they can't be repaired. Stretch pants are $55, jerseys $35. Shoulder and hip pads go for $80. Chest and back plates cost $220 since they have to be custom molded to each player. Leggins and arm guards are $65. Kidney protectors cost us $35. Chain mail is another $50.

We supply each player with two pairs of shoes. This amounts to $60. He also gets five pairs of snap-on soles, one each for ice, hot asphalt, concrete, snow and all-purpose general. These cost us an additional $25. Thermal underwear, gloves, socks and other miscellaneous stuff like that sets us back another $30.

Traveling outfits, team capes and coveralls set us back $150 per man.

We don't have to provide iron horses and supporters, though. In this department, every man takes care of himself.

In the weapons area, our long knives cost us $130 each, including sheaths. That's because we have them specially balanced and honed. The handles and blades are constructed out of one-piece dura-steel. The guard is set into place by a special hot-forging process. The handles are wrapped in non-slip rubber. We strip the handles and rewrap them after every game because blood and sweat has a tendency to soak into them and stiffen them up. The sheaths are made of self-lubricating plastic. They'll stay pliable and slippery for the quick draw from 20 degrees below zero up to 115 degrees.

The bleeders we have made by an English company that got its start making razor blades. Here, too, the blade is a part of the handle, but, to make sure we stay legal with regard to amount of blade exposure, so is the guard. The handles are wrapped the same way as the long knives. The sheaths are constructed the same way, too. The bleeders and their sheaths cost us $95 each.

Short clubs are the cheapest weapon we have. They're only $60 each counting their clip. That's because they're so simple to make. The clubs and the clips are injection molded out of plastic. The thongs are nylon. From what they tell me, the guys who make them can knock them out at the rate of about one every ten minutes. Nothing to it.

The bolas go for $105. They're made of three steel balls, vacuum dropped up there in space in SkyFac to make sure they're perfectly round. Then they're encased in plastic and hooked together with thin nylon cord. Altogether, the whole thing weighs in at less than four pounds.

Not many players carry the javelins, but we keep some in stock, anyway. They're made of lightweight tubular alloy and are steel-tipped. The handles are rubber-wrapped. They cost us $80 each.

We don't have to worry about the cost of the hidden safety's rifle, since rifle companies provide us those for free. If I had to put a price tag on them, though, I'd say it probably costs about $450–$500 to make one.

We've also got a lot of hidden expenses that nobody ever seems to think about. Tape, for instance. At the beginning of a season, when a man's fairly tight, each guy gets wound with maybe four rolls of aluminum, three rolls of surgical. Toward the end of the year, when a man is more prone to injury, we double the amount of surgical tape. (We still use four rolls of aluminum, though.) Our tape bill for the season averages out to roughly $300 per man.

We have eighty-two specially decorated traveling trunks that we use to carry equipment to away games. (You talk about a job. Manhandling those trunks around is one of the worst there is. They're heavy going out, but they're even heavier coming back. Every man's uniform picks up roughly eight pounds worth of sweat during a game.) The trunks cost $600 each.

We also change shoelaces before every game. If a man's shoelace breaks during a crucial series and his shoe falls off, that's one more vulnerable area of his body exposed, not to mention a loss of mobility. Shoelaces are cheap, but you buy enough of them and it all adds up—$20 per man for shoelaces every year.

It costs us $80,000 in flight insurance every time we fly to an away game. (The team is insured for $90,000,000.) Our average cost for airplane tickets is $60,000 per flight, and you have to add the Environmental Protection Agency's 10 per cent sur-charge, or $6,000, on top of that.

While it varies, up and down, depending on where we play

and how rough the action gets, I'd say we wind up paying off maybe around $500,000 in damage claims after every game.

We've also got to spring for the cost of evacuating residents from the playing area and keeping up the displacement villages. Figure $60,000,000 a year for that.

Then there's the players' salaries. They vary, but the average is somewhere around $550,000 per man per year.

Last but not least is the football itself. It costs us $35, and for every home game we have to provide 24 new ones. The footballs are a standard league item made by Spaulding, who calls them "The SFL Special." They're exactly 11¼ inches long, 21½ inches in circumference. They're made out of a special weatherproof Naugahyde with a nubbly texture to make them feel like leather. (Footballs used to be called "pigskins" but were really made out of cowhide. The current lack of cows makes that pretty impractical nowadays.) The lacings are made of the same stuff. We make it a practice to give the touchdown ball to the man who scored it, a custom that's starting to catch on with other teams in the league.

So there you've got it. Cough up maybe ninety, maybe one hundred million dollars' worth of seed money, and you too can field your own professional street football team.

Me, I'll stick with the one I've got.

(Herb Carrerra, *Run to Midnight* [Miami: Gridiron Press, 2004], pp. 34–38)

Monday, March 15, 2010

"Two twenty-six. T.K., you're no fun at all," says the Prospectors' team physician. "You're as consistent as my old maiden aunt's bowel movements. I don't think your weight's varied a pound in the ten years I've been with the team." The doctor taps a brown manila folder against the scale. "Your other tests all look good. You're in disgustingly perfect health."

"I owe it to fast living and Clasp toothpaste," joshes T.K., aping a Harv Matision TV commercial currently showing around. He steps off the scale, retrieves his practice pads from a bench against the wall and slips them on.

There are sixty-eight men scattered around the locker room; twenty-five are rookies. Since it's only a practice, and an early one at that, the team hasn't yet worked up to full armor. Instead, all are dressed in sponge rubber chest and back pads, blue shorts, rubber knee and elbow pads, and flat-soled rubber shoes. All wear a training suit, a piece of apparel that duplicates the weight distribution of a set of football armor. At this point in their training, most players carry only around thirty pounds. Before the season starts, they'll all be up to eighty-pound suits, nearly twice as much weight as they'll have to carry in a game, but Coach Carrerra is big on conditioning. The team's rookies are required to wear their training suits twenty-four hours a day until the first game. Invariably, a fanatical veteran or two will join them. Everyone there either carries, wears or is within reaching distance of a blue plastic practice helmet emblazoned with a gold letter P.

The rookies are a sullen, introspective bunch. They don't talk much, not to the veterans at all, hardly to each other. All have been drafted straight out of college, the last bastion of field style football, so they've never played street football. They've got a lot to learn. Their first task is to pick up enough to make the team—by the start of the season, the roster will be cut to fifty-two men. Their next, and most important, chore is to learn how to stay alive once they get in a game.

The veterans, on the other hand, are quite jovial. They banter freely, joke and laugh. They don't waste their energy getting psyched up for practice. Nobody ever gets killed in practice. The knives are rubber, the bullets blanks. They save their solemnity, their single-minded concentration for actual games. That's where it really makes the difference.

T.K. takes a seat on the floor near Eddie Hougart, the team's halfback/deep safety. Eddie is T.K.'s best friend. Rooming together in college started it. Saving each other's hides in countless games solidified it. Eddie is big and loose. His stomach hangs out over his belt, his legs and arms jiggle when he walks.

He gives the impression that his bulk is all fat. Nothing could be further from the truth. T.K.'s hit him often enough in practice to know that flab covers a nucleus of solid muscle.

Eddie is the team flake, a regular clown. He delights in practical jokes which usually involve such questionably humorous acts as throwing a rookie out a second-story hotel window or secretly rubbing heating compound into a teammate's supporter just prior to the start of a fifty-mile run. Eddie carries a collection of pornography around in his billfold. Most of it he has taken out and displayed so often it's become ripped, worn and unreadable. Eddie doesn't seem to notice, or care. He keeps dragging it out again, anyway, blissfully unconcerned that most of the people he shows it to have already seen it, often several times.

"Take a look at this." Eddie winks as he pulls a soiled piece of film out of his locker. "Ain't that the shits."

T.K., who has seen this particular item maybe fifty times before, obligingly takes it, anyway, and holds it up to the light. It's an X-ray shot of a limp penis with a broken bone depicted inside. "That's some injury you got there, Eddie," T.K. says, handing the X-ray back. "You ought to see the doc about a splint."

"Yeah, a splint. That's good. I like that." Eddie holds the X-ray at arm's length.

"So do I," T.K. says, sadly watching his friend squint down his arm at the photo. Eddie, like T.K., is getting old. But while T.K. is physically in good shape, Eddie Hougart is not. For the past several seasons, he's been slowly losing his eyesight. He has several different sets of contact lenses, one set for sunny days, one for nighttime, one for snow glare, one for rain, et cetera. But even they don't sharpen his eyesight as well as it should be. How does he play football, then? He mainly goes on instinct. And guts. As long as his instinct and his guts hold out, he'll have a place on the team. When they go, so does he, one way or another.

Coach Carrerra enters the locker room. He's a man of few words and gets right down to business. "We'll have offensive drills and unarmed combat practice this morning. Primary positions. Quarterbacks with me. Halfbacks and fullbacks with Coach Johnson. Centers, guards, tackles with Coach Fernandez. Ends with Coach Miller. And don't forget your play books. Hidden safeties, you'll be spending the whole day with Coach Leicht at the rifle range. For the defensive drills and weapons sessions this afternoon, free and deep safeties and middle linebackers with me, Coach Stassen and Coach Ralan. Linemen and ends with Coach Immura. Zack"—Zack Rauscher is the Prospectors' mediman—"I've got you set up to spend the day at Stanford studying with Doc Zimmerman and his orthopedic group."

T.K. notes his assignments. He'll be with Coach Carrerra both morning and afternoon. In street football, where there are no substitutions, every man plays both offense and defense. On defense, T.K.'s primary position is free safety. (Sooner or later before the actual start of the season, he as well as every other man on the team will also get secondary cross training in every other position, both offensive and defensive, as well. This so that in the event of an injury or a death, players can, at the quarterback's discretion, switch around between positions.)

The Prospectors practice on a run-down street in an industrial section of Hunter's Point, an area just south of San Francisco. It's an ideal practice area. It doesn't get much traffic, there are some fairly good-sized buildings for use in vertical wind sprints, there are few, if any, people living there, and except for the early morning and late evening rush hours, the street is almost deserted.

Coach Carrerra takes T.K. and his two backup quarterbacks, a four-year veteran named Halloran and a rookie named Tross, who was the talk of the Big Ten last year, out to the goalyard, a line three feet long with upright poles implanted on each end. This is the line that must be crossed for a touchdown.

"I've been working on this new maneuver," he tells them, "for goalyard penetration, and I want your opinions before I put it in the play book. This is it." He puts one of his mechanical blocking dummies in front of the yard. Coach Carrerra is hooked on technology. He never uses a plain steel and cotton dummy if there's a mechanical one that will do the same job.

The situation he sets up, the goalyard with one defender standing in front of it, is a relatively common situation in street football, seen quite often in a game. Having a man on the yard virtually guarantees one last chance to prevent penetration, but it also negates the effectiveness of the hidden safety since he can't use his gun if there's a defensive man between the ball carrier and the goalyard.

Coach Carrerra's mechanical dummy shuffles back and forth, wheezing with rugged authenticity. The coach stuffs a football into the gut pocket of his sweat shirt. "This is it. I call it my crab around. Coming straight at the defender, you hook into him with a cross body block, thusly." He demonstrates on the dummy, taking care to first turn it down to less than one-quarter power. He coaches football, he doesn't play it. "Then you slide off the man's hip, crabwise like this, keeping him turned to the outside. You spin around him across the line." He crosses the line and straightens up. "What do you think?" He is obviously quite proud of his new movement.

"I'll have to think about it," says Halloran, who plays his football the same way he does his life, as noncommittally as possible.

"I think it's great," says Tross, who doesn't really understand it but figures he might as well get in some brownie points whenever he can.

"It's shitty," says T.K., advancing toward the dummy. The dummy takes a menacing stance, so T.K. shuts it off. "Try it with me," he tells Coach Carrerra.

The coach comes at him, throws the cross body, and starts his crab around. In that instant, T.K. grabs his coach under the chin, and jerks his head back, using Carrerra's own motion against him. He lets up short of doing any real damage. "Your theory is good, but a sharp defender will take a guy's head off, helmet and all, on a move like that. I still prefer either a two-on-one if you can get it, or a running butt." In the first technique, one offensive man battles the goalyard's defender while the ball carrier crosses the line. It works more often than it doesn't, but it's somewhat hard to set up, what with its necessitating that two offensive players shake their defensive coverage. The second, the running butt, is a straight-on head-down run at the defender, a strategy that may carry both the ball carrier and the defender across the goalyard together, or may break the ball carrier's neck. In street football, there are pros and cons to everything.

Coach Carrerra's not really disappointed with his theory's washout. In fact, he knew it would fail all along. But he had to see which of his quarterbacks knew it, too, and which would be ballsy enough to tell him so. While the quarterback picks the team, the coach picks the quarterback. It's one of the few controls he has. The head office has been after Carrerra for months to start someone younger, to start Tross. From time to time Coach Carrerra likes to pull a stunt like this, solely to reassure himself that, head office opinions to the contrary, the youngest man isn't necessarily the best man, too.

For the afternoon session, T.K. takes his long knife, the weapon carried by all safety men and linebackers. In practice, plays are run with rubber knives, not real ones, but Coach Carrerra likes to put his men through some actual stabbing practice, usually on a cotton dummy, to give them the feel of their armament. As a safety, T.K.'s also entitled to carry either a bola or a five-foot-long spear. He carries the bola. A spear is next to worthless against armor, and it's awkward to handle, besides. T.K. doesn't bother bringing along his bleeder. Most of his defensive work is run and pursuit, and in that kind of action, he doesn't have much use for it, not like the linemen, who use it constantly.

T.K. stops in the john on the way out. When he finally gets to the street, the linebackers are practicing with their short clubs. The clubs are six inches long, suspended from twelve-inch nylon thongs. The linebackers put in two or three minutes on strangling practice, an equal amount of time on beating drill.

T.K. hustles over to where Coach Carrerra is standing with the safeties. He's the last to arrive. "You men," says Coach Carrerra, motioning to the linebackers, "over here." The linebackers double-time over. Coach Carrerra addresses the entire group, safeties and linebackers together. "You men have got to learn to use your long knives effectively. You've got six inches of weapon there, the most potent tactical weapon in the football arsenal, and you've got to learn to use it effectively."

". . . to use it effectively," harmonizes Eddie Hougart, who has prodigiously memorized Coach Carrerra's entire book, *Run to Midnight,* not so as to improve his play but to needle the coach for his frequently repetitious admonitions.

T.K. catches a whiff of something foul, and glances over his shoulder to see an approaching herd of goats. There must be fifty of them. It's starting to look like a tough afternoon.

"For you rookies," explains Coach Carrerra, "this is called goat drill. It has a twofold purpose. It teaches you to use your long knife effectively, and it gets you used to the sight of blood. What we do is to let one of these animals loose. What you do is you catch it and you kill it. Quickly, and neatly, with no wasted motion. O.K. First man out."

The first man in line, a rookie, lets his goat get away. Coach Carrerra gives him fifty laps. The second man, a six-year veteran, catches his goat and dispatches it in one fluid motion.

"Look at that, you men," shouts the coach, "just look at the way he did that. That's the way I want you all to do it. Quickly, neatly, with no wasted motion."

T.K. takes his turn, quickly, neatly, with no wasted motion.

After each goat is slaughtered, a team of coaching assistants drags its carcass to a nearby pushcart and dumps it inside. After practice, the goats will be wheeled into the kitchen of the team's cafeteria, where they will be dressed out. Meat is scarce, and Coach Carrerra is thrifty. Goat will be a training table staple for the next two weeks.

Afterwards, when there are no goats left, using rubber knives this time, the safeties and linebackers practice stabbing techniques on each other.

Through with the afternoon session, the players sit around the locker room waiting for the coach to begin the team meeting.

As usual, the hidden safeties, Gus D'Armato, the first stringer and two rookies, sit off to one side by themselves. The hidden safety is practically always the most withdrawn, the most introverted member of the team. The rules of the game go a long way toward making him so. In addition to his rifle and one bullet, he's permitted an unlimited number of knives of any type he wishes so long as no one of his blades exceeds twenty-four inches. Most hidden safeties opt for long-bladed butcher knives or machetes. This combination of firepower and cutlery makes the hidden safety a very potent defensive force, but there's a counterbalance to his power. Long knives can be used only against two players, the ball carrier and the hidden safety. Hence, the hidden safety is the only member of the team who can be attacked and killed on sight.

Their backgrounds—hidden safeties are usually recruited from among the ranks of ex-convicts, gangsters, army snipers, anyone who has a ready familiarity with weapons—and their peculiar dual status as both hunter and hunted conspire to make the hidden safeties the team loners. While the other players relax, drink beer or joke around, the hidden safeties patiently clean and polish their rifles or sharpen their knives. To them, football is more than a game. It's a total way of life.

Coach Carrerra comes in. "Men," he says, launching into what the veterans instantly recognize as the beginnings of a pep talk. "This year, we're going all the way. Straight to the top." With seven slashes, he puts a Roman numeral on the blackboard. "Whenever you're out there on the street, whenever you're running, or blocking, or shooting, or fighting, I want you to remember where it's all leading up to. Concentrate on reaching this number. This is our goal. This is the number of the Superbowl that we're going to win."

The blackboard reads XXI.

Sunday, March 21, 2010

Nobody likes Koko Hofsteder's parties. Her caterer makes abominable hors d'oeuvres, her bartender pours short shots, her pusher supplies her with diluted drugs. And Koko's repartee consists of two parts vanity, one part sycophantism.

Yet, banal and witless though they may be, Koko Hofsteder's parties are always well attended by the cream of Washington society. Senators, representatives, justices, all make an appearance, because, by inferred mutual consent, Koko Hofsteder's parties have come to be a sort of neutral zone, a place to discuss political positioning, to give fair warning, to unveil a threat.

The party has been in full swing for almost an hour, and the pleasantries of social etiquette are rapidly being replaced by the affairs of state, a caucus in the kitchen, a collusion in the den.

Threading his way through the smoky web of parliamentary jargon, Senator Lako Barin approaches Senator Cy Abelman.

"Cy, good to see you," he says with an orator's measured resonance, his voice wrapped in the protective shroud of a hundred other ongoing conversations.

Senator Abelman, busy gnawing on a piece of white bread topped with an unrecognizable, basically tasteless spread, bobs his head once to acknowledge his colleague's presence, then resumes his eating, choosing mediocre food over Lako Barin's conversation.

The affront isn't lost on Barin, who counters it with a rare display of levity. "When you finish your sandwich, I recommend the drug table. Koko's serving a superb bicarbonate of soda."

In spite of himself, Abelman chuckles, but it's not a signal of mirth, it's the venting of tension that so often precedes the deadly serious business of confrontation. He sets his plate aside, wipes his hands on his coat. "Very well, Senator. Let's get it over with. I'll give you my stand in the most straightforward of terms. I find your street football bill not only reprehensible but also morally obscene. I'll do everything in my power, take every conceivable action, pull every available string to see it defeated." Abelman's an old man, prone, on occasion, to loosen the cork of maturity that usually bottles up his emotions. When he finishes speaking, his face is a window depicting the choleric fury inside him.

Rather than accepting Abelman's statement at face value as a sincere demarcation of a man's belief, Barin takes it as a negotiable demand in the collective bargaining that commonly passes for political integrity. "Cy, I don't think I need remind you. I'm in a position to do you a lot of good. Harriman owes me a rather large favor. I can cash it in to spring your mass transit bill out of committee. Or that parks and forests thing you're so set on enacting. I can assure you of passage. Just tell me what you want, and it's yours."

"All right." Abelman nods briskly, setting up wispy currents in his long, sparse white hair. "Gladly. I'll tell you what I want. I want an end to legalized murder. Instead of giving football players more weapons, I want them disarmed completely."

"Now, Cy, you sound like one of those End Blood Sports people. Next thing I know, you'll be parading around outside my office with a placard and a list of dead athletes." Barin steps in closer, warming to the battle. "Come off your high horse, Cy. Street football is no passing fancy. It's the most popular sport in the world, the most popular sport ever. Hop on the bandwagon while there's still room."

Abelman doesn't back away, literally or figuratively. "Senator, you and your media cohorts are turning this country into a perversive nation of depraved, voyeuristic ghouls. I want no part whatsoever in serving up bloodshed for breakfast, death for dinner and a smidgen of torture with tea."

"Splendid alliteration, Cy, a linguistic *tour de force,* but a bit on the sensational side. The actual facts are quite to the contrary. My media friends and I are simply giving the American people what they want. Exciting entertainment. You act as though I'm trying to equip football teams with machine guns or bazookas, for goodness sakes. When all I want to do is provide football's hidden safety with four bullets instead of one. Do you honestly think giving one man three more bullets can pervert a nation?"

"No, not pervert. Destroy."

Senator Barin gives forth a round, hearty laugh. "I can make it worth your while to come over to my side, Cy. I can help you a lot. Keep that in mind. Or I can hurt you. I can do that, too."

Abelman puckers up his lips and crinkles his nose. "You make me want to puke," he says in decidedly non-diplomatic fashion.

A shrill, squeaky voice cuts short Senator Barin's renewed laughter. "Friends," screeches Koko Hofsteder in that breathless way she uses to announce the arrival of yet another important dignitary. "Here's someone I just know you'll all want to meet." She habitually introduces her guests with the slam-bang come-on of a TV talk show hostess. "A most prominent figure in the sporting arena, the winner of the last Superbowl, as cute in person as he is on the TV screen, Harv Matision."

Matision swaggers into the room. He's dressed completely in white, a white leather headband, white cape, white silk shirt open to the navel, white doeskin pants, white boots. Around his middle he sports the white belt and six-inch gold buckle of a Superbowl winner. He has with him an albino German shepherd. The dog snarls at the assemblage. So does Matision. Koko Hofsteder squeals with delight, takes Matision by the arm and escorts him into the throng.

Lako Barin hurries over to the two of them. "Harv, good to see you again. Great performance you put on in the Superbowl."

"If you think that was good, wait 'til you see me in the next one." No modesty in Harv Matision.

The *Times* society photographer lines up a shot of the two talking. Senator Barin, sensing the photographer's presence, turns his strong profile to the camera. The photographer catches it, as Senator Barin pays him to. He also catches Koko Hofsteder with her mouth open, and Senator Cy Abelman looking disgusted in the background. A minor retouch in his darkroom takes Koko completely out of the picture, and puts a distinctly drunken leer of envy on Abelman's face.

The shot runs on page twelve in the morning edition.

SUPERBOWL XXI, THE GAME

Saturday, January 1, 2011, 12:00 Midnight

T.K. kicks off, a booming shot traveling straight down Myrtle almost to Irving. He has Pfleg, Frazier, Minick, Brye and Clausen lined up to his left, Dedemus, DeGeller, Michalski, Healy and Howe to his right. Since Myrtle is quite narrow, they're less than an arm's length apart. Rauscher is pressed up against a bank around the corner and out of the way on Anderson. D'Armato is on the top floor of an office building on Mt. Vernon.

The Minutemen's deep receiver takes the kick, jogs right onto Irving, and cuts into an apartment house.

T.K. dodges his blocker and turns down Garden, the street one over west from Irving. From his scouting endeavors of the days before, T.K. remembers that the apartment house the ball carrier went into has entrances on both streets. Sure enough, no sooner does T.K. reach the Garden Street entrance than the ball carrier comes charging out.

Almost without thinking, T.K. unfurls his bola and heaves it. It wraps tightly around the ball carrier's legs, sending him sprawling to the pavement.

The referee blows his whistle into his amplifier, and, through his transmitter, conveys to the other referees the fact that the play has ended.

Led by the referees, the members of both teams make their way to Garden Street.

T.K. takes a quick survey. On the kickoff, DeGeller suffered some bleeder bites, Healy twisted an ankle. Both are able to keep playing. All told, the Prospectors came out of the kickoff in very good shape. But then, so did the opposition. The Minutemen line up thirteen strong, as well.

On the first play of the game, Matision throws a short, swing pass to his end out in the flat.

With a traditional flying tackle, Michalski stops it for a short gain.

The next play is a keeper. Matision swings left and charges hard up Revere. T.K. and Frazier gang tackle him. Howe and Clausen pile on before the whistle blows. Everybody, it seems, is swinging a knife.

Matision gets up unmarked and laughing.

On third down, Matision sends his fullback plowing into the line. At this stage of the game, with both sides fully manned, it's a stupid maneuver. It's smothered at the line for no gain.

With fourth down coming up, the Minutemen need nearly forty yards for a first down. T.K. hangs back to take the punt.

The Minutemen break their huddle, come up to the line, set in punt formation, then switch to a standard long-stem T, quarterback five yards behind center, with a halfback to either side, the fullback split wide.

"They're going for it," T.K. yells, hustling back into position.

Matision takes the ball, and cuts around right end. He's down Anderson to Myrtle, Myrtle to Grove before anyone can so much as touch him. At that point, he has the first down easily, but he's not through, yet.

He smashes into a dry cleaning store and out the other side, swings up a fire escape and loses his pursuit across the darkened rooftops. He comes down on Revere and there encounters his first real opposition.

Buddy Healy overtakes him from the side. Matision gives him a stiff-arm and tries to fake around him. Healy isn't buying it, though. He hits Matision straight on, his short club flying.

Forbidden to use any weapons save his hands while on offense, Matision slams a chop at Healy's neck. Healy slides partially under it, but it still connects with enough force to drive him down and to the side. Matision takes advantage of Healy's awkward positioning. He swings his steel-toed boot around, landing it squarely in Healy's groin. Healy doubles over, but his legs keep churning. No matter. Matision slams him in the groin, again. Healy goes down. For good measure, Matision kicks him in the groin three more times and heads for the goalyard, located on Cedar between Revere and Pinckney.

When he realizes Matision has given them the slip, T.K.

sends Minick to act as goalyard tender. T.K. and all those Prospectors able to do so, shake their opponents and assume a zone coverage, trying to locate Matision before he can get into scoring position.

They're too late, though. Matision is already at the goalyard. Minick tries to fend him off with his short club, but Matision is too quick for him. The Minutemen quarterback dives in low. Minick swings, misses, and Matision slams into his knees, breaking one and tearing the cartilage in the other.

The referee signals a touchdown.

The point after has to be made from thirty-five yards out. Matision gives to his halfback. The halfback gets creamed at the goalyard, but he laterals to the center, who comes in after him, standing up.

The referee blows his whistle.

Score: Minutemen 7, Prospectors 0.

Elapsed time: Forty-six minutes.

Casualties: Minutemen, none.

Prospectors, Buddy Healy red-crossed for at least an hour with a badly swollen groin, Harland Minick out for the rest of the game.

T.K. lines up to take the kickoff. It's shaping up as a very rough day.

Thursday, April 29, 2010

T.K. and Eddie Hougart share a pedicab home from practice.

The cabman, unaccustomed to pedaling around such massive specimens of humanity, poops out noticeably on the uphill grades, but more than compensates for it by picking up an alarming head of steam on the way down, a dichotomy of motion which imbues the ride with all the stomach-lurching characteristics of a trip on a roller coaster.

His passengers, though, are much too fatigued to complain, or even to care, for that matter.

Scrunched down in the seat to keep his head from brushing the cab's canvas top, Eddie polishes off his usual after-practice, pre-dinner snack, a hundred capsules of protein supplement, fifty steroid tablets. T.K. catnaps.

The cabman pulls over to the curb outside a shabby building on Montgomery Street. Ted Monreves, T.K.'s business agent, has his office here. The building was once a very prestigious address, but prestige has long ago moved out to the suburbs with everyone else. As T.K.'s popularity, and, by extension, Ted Monreves' commissions, faded, they both found themselves marching in place, T.K. in time to a coach's cadence, Monreves to the bay of bill collectors. Neither has, as yet, found a suitable way to change stride.

Monreves had buzzed T.K. at home this morning to set up a meeting for after practice. Apparently, Monreves had arranged some sort of business deal for T.K. Although this shouldn't have surprised T.K.—after all, that was Monreves' job—it did. Aging quarterbacks weren't getting the nod for endorsements, talk shows or lectures any more, only for a life's worth of hell on a street every Sunday.

"Want to come up?" T.K. asks Eddie. "We can grab some beers after."

Eddie shrugs. "Might as well. Beats going home to the old lady."

T.K. pays off the cabman, and climbs out.

"Ain't you T.K. Mann?" asks a small boy wearing a Minutemen jersey with 69, Harv Matision's number, on it. Emulating the professionals, the boy has mock scars painted on his neck and both wrists, a very popular faddish affectation lately, even among boys well into their teens.

"Sure am," admits T.K., expecting to be asked for an autograph.

"Bang, you're dead," screams the boy, pointing both hands, index fingers extended, in T.K.'s direction. "That's what Harv Matision's gonna do to you this season. He's gonna shoot you dead."

"Thanks for the warning," says T.K., turning his back on the boy.

"Bang," shouts the boy after him, "bang, bang, bang, bang."

"Come in, T.K.," says Ted, holding open the door. The gesture gives T.K. some indication of this deal's importance to Monreves. He hasn't opened a door for T.K. in nearly five years, ever since a mutual decline in prosperity dulled the distinction between agent and client. "There's someone I'd like you to meet."

"We've already met," says Sarah Lauffler, the girl from the Pro-Am Golf Tournament in Atlanta. Idly puffing a pipe, she sits comfortably in the last vestige of Ted's salad years, a fluffy overstuffed chair.

"Miss Lauffler," says T.K. "Kind of far from home, aren't you? How's your brother?"

"Nonexistent," she replies. "I must apologize to you for my charade in Atlanta, but you see I wanted to meet you informally. It was quite important that I get a feel for your true character before you found out what I do and erected a misleading facade."

"And what exactly is it you do?"

Ted answers for her. "She's going to do a long feature article on you, T.K. For a national magazine."

"Oh, really? Which one?"

"*EBS*," says Sarah bluntly before Ted has a chance to couch a more gradational reply.

"Ted, you're kidding me." T.K. spreads his hands out imploringly from his sides. "That's the magazine of the End Blood Sports group. They've been against street football from the day it was born. There's no way that magazine's going to print anything positive about me. I won't do it. I can get all the adverse publicity I want on my own."

"T.K.," Ted answers, "Miss Lauffler has assured me she's not interested in deliberate character assassination. She wants to do a straightforward personality profile of a professional street football player. If it turns out to be flattering, which in your

case I don't see how else it could, that's the way she'll write it.
And I believe her. Honestly, T.K., I don't think you've got a
thing to worry about."

"Damn right I don't, because I'm not going to do it."

"I'm afraid you don't have any choice." Ted spreads open his
hands the same way T.K. had. Imploringly. "I've already
signed the contract. Back out, and EBS can sue us both for
what little we've got left."

Ted turns his back to T.K. "I've got a wife and three kids,
T.K. I've got medical bills, food bills, clothing bills, the rent's
coming due. EBS paid me cash on the line."

T.K.'s not angry. He's let Ted Monreves handle his business
dealings long enough to know Monreves wouldn't deliberately
sell him out, no matter what the price. If Ted made the deal, he
did it because he honestly believed that, at the worst, it would
do T.K. no harm. T.K. nods. "O.K., so I'm going to be the cen-
terfold in EBS. What the hell do I care about my image, anyway?" He reflects for a moment before posing a question to
Sarah. "Why me? Why not Matision or one of the younger
guys?"

Her frankness is bluntly revealing. "Two reasons. First, you
were the only famous player I could persuade to do it."

T.K. throws a dirty look at Ted which Ted does his best to
pretend he doesn't see. "And the other reason?"

"Your type of man fascinates me."

For a moment, her totally unexpected admission leaves T.K.
at a loss for words, but only for a moment. "So you're attracted
to old men and losers," he says through a jovial grin.

She tilts her head, as if it lets her view his statement from a
different perspective. "That's exactly what interests me about
you. Not the part about old men and losers. You're certainly
neither of those. No, it's something else, something I noticed in
you in Atlanta and again, here, now. You're so terribly hard on
yourself. You seem to have an amazingly low regard for your
abilities and, I sense, for your profession as well. I don't see
how you can survive, let alone excel, in street football feeling
the way that you do."

"I'm only kidding."

"I don't think so."

"Well, I guess you'll have lots of time to find out. When do we start?"

"How about tomorrow morning?"

"Super. Practice starts at six A.M."

"I'll be there."

"Great. Bring your camera. As a special exclusive to the readers of *EBS*, I'll demonstrate some of the more humane forms of hand-to-hand killing."

Without waiting for her reply, he collects Eddie and leaves.

Sunday, May 2, 2010

"There's the kickoff," announces Timothy Enge, "and that starts another great season of SFL action."

Jaime and Surdo Sakura watch this, the first game of the year, a hard-fought contest between the San Francisco Prospectors and the Honolulu Sharks, from a spacious one-bedroom displacement home on Maui.

The game is being played on Oahu, in Honolulu, and its boundaries encompass the high-rise apartment house on Walinea Street in which the Sakuras reside. The official SFL playing area is 700 yards by 350 yards, approximately eight blocks by four, although it can be slightly more, or less, subject to the exact layout of the streets concerned. Depending on the precise location of the streets selected, this usually means that anywhere from ten to one hundred thousand people will have to be evacuated, given a one-day football vacation as the SFL dulcetly phrases it. The SFL teams have become quite adept at large-scale transportation. Special trams ferry the vacationeers, as they're called, from their homes to the homes away from home the teams have set up. There they spend game day relaxing, eating, drinking or drugging at SFL expense. Most of the displaced forgo the free golf courses, the free banquets, the free dances, the free movies, the free bowling alleys and tennis courts, however, in favor of watching on TV the game that has displaced them. Each house in the village is equipped with a jumbo fifty-inch full-color TV set, a considerable improvement over the thirty-inchers common to most homes and apartments. But the sheer size of the set is only one of the attractions of watching the game in the village. The SFL gratuitously provides all viewers with an unlimited number of free replays. What with the cost of living being as high as it is and the relatively little extra money most people have available to spend on replays, this is a very welcome benefit, indeed, and one which vastly overshadows the multitude of other pleasures the village has to offer. So appealing is this benefit, in fact, that almost never does a resident of a playing area refuse to move out of his own free will. (If he does, he is, of course, transported by force. The games must go on.)

For Jaime, who sells patio covers and pedals a cab part time, and Surdo, who works as an information retrieval operator for a local insurance company, the situation affords an all too rare relief from the financial considerations which usually severely limit the extent of their viewing.

They arise at 11 P.M. on Saturday, a full hour before kickoff. So as to make certain they don't miss a single play throughout the day, they fortify themselves with amphetamines, which the Sharks have thoughtfully left for them in large bottles in the medicine cabinet.

As the game progresses, they watch every moment, hour after hour, dashing to the bathroom and the kitchen only during the quarter time-outs, watching replays during the commercials (which still doesn't save them from being exposed to a sales pitch since every replay is, itself, preceded by an abridged commercial).

The game is nearly over.

The Sharks are losing, the Prospectors have the ball. Then, on third down and short yardage, Eddie Hougart, the Prospectors' halfback/deep safety, fumbles. The Sharks' center recovers. Since a ball turnover such as occurs with a fumble or an interception alters which team has the use of weapons, runbacks are prohibited. The ball is immediately blown dead, giving the Sharks possession on Nahua Street, the Prospectors' 320 yard line. Danny Ho, the Sharks' quarterback, a Hawaiian native, and thusly an adored local hero, takes the snap and keeps it. In a brilliant turn around left end, he ducks into a department store, where he shakes his pursuers. He makes his way out to Kuhio Street and has almost reached Seaside Avenue and the Prospectors' goalyard, when he's intercepted by a deep safety and a lineman. Circling warily, they trap him between them. Acting quickly, before defensive reinforcements arrive, Danny tucks the ball into his gut pocket and engages the deep safety, who, with his long knife, is easily the more dangerous of the two. The lineman immediately assaults Danny from the rear with his short club, but Ho pays him no more attention than an elephant would an attack from a flea.

The light-intensifying TV cameras recording the scene catch and amplify every tiny bit of illumination so the battle can be seen as clearly as if it were being fought in broad daylight. So true are the colors, so clear the action, the only way to tell this is not happening during the daytime is by the strange, surreal fact none of the combatants casts a shadow.

The deep safety jockeys for a clear and killing shot under Ho's helmet, at his neck, but Ho is a wary and experienced ballplayer. He keeps his chin well down, his neck covered. Abruptly, Ho makes his move. He catches the deep safety's arm under his own. With a twisting motion, he breaks it at the elbow. The deep safety gamely tries to switch his knife to his other hand, but Ho is already way out of his reach, doing battle with the lineman. The lineman has Ho in a bear hug, and is beating on his kidneys from behind. Gambling, Ho drops to one knee. In a beautiful clean and jerk, made all the more difficult by the angle through which he has to execute it, Ho picks up the lineman in both hands and raises him into the air. Squatting down again, he slams the hapless lineman over his braced and upraised knee. The man's back breaks with a gratifying snap. Ho rises and sprints for the goalyard, using a running butt against the goalyard tender to carry himself across.

Jaime and Surdo go wild, rerunning the sequence a giddily thriftless four times, once each from all four viewpoints, Ho's, the lineman's, the deep safety's and the goalyard tender's.

Ho takes in the extra point himself, but it's a fruitless gesture.

T.K. Mann has called a flawless game, and the Sharks lose, 93 to 80.

"Wow," says Jaime, helping Surdo return their personal belongings to their suitcase for the trip back to their apartment. "What a finish! It'll take me all day tomorrow to recuperate from it."

"Me too," Surdo agrees, still noticeably flushed and slightly out of breath even though the game has been over for nearly an hour.

"I live for the start of football season," muses Jaime. "I don't know what I'd do if I couldn't watch the games."

"I guess we'd be bored to tears," suggests Surdo.

"I guess we would."

A tram pulls up to start them on the first leg of their journey home.

International Broadcasting Company, IBC Building, 200 Fifth Avenue, New York, New York 10016

INTEROFFICE

To: Pierce Spencer
From: Ida Moulay, Vice-President in Charge of Programming
Date: May 3, 2010

NOTE—This memo is company private and is printed on flash paper. It will disintegrate if photocopied or if allowed to remain outside its protective envelope for longer than five minutes.

Just a note to let you know the football player recruiting program is an unqualified success. Every player on the list you approved was signed up and equipped in time for the opening game on Sunday.

As an interesting aside, even though we had only two men

(one on each team) under our guidance in each contest, still we were quite easily able to successfully dictate the action levels of every game played. I believe this conclusively confirms your theory.

I feel we may now start to think in terms of our longer-range goals, to wit, (a) the creation of "ideal" or "dream" matches to boost ratings, (b) the continued build-up of a "bigger than life" hero (Harv Matision has worked out quite well thus far—depending on your eventual objectives, we may want to stick with him) to be used for network promotional purposes, and (c) the elimination of players who don't contribute to the excitement of the game (T.K. Mann comes immediately to mind—perhaps a "dream" match pitting him against Matision in which Mann emerges the hapless, i.e., lifeless, victim?). I leave these suggestions for your consideration.

For your information, I'm enclosing the directoral transcript from a representative play in one of yesterday's games. Brief though it may be, I feel it will adequately enable you to evaluate the performance of Danny Ho. A recent acquisition, he seems to be working out quite nicely. We may want to keep him in mind for future stardom.

Should you have any questions, I'll be only too happy to answer them.

IM/cc   ENCLOSURE
                                    Directoral Transcript

Directoral Transcript, Sharks versus Prospectors, May 2, 2010

Excerpt

Audio (Programming Coordinator to Danny Ho)	Audio (on-the-air broadcast)
Keep it. The defensive call is a blitz right. You take it around left end you can shake 'em.	Danny Ho takes the snap, and gallops around left end in a brilliant evasive maneuver.

Cut out to Kuhio Street and make for Seaside Avenue. Don't bother to sneak. It's clear all the way.

What a gambler this Ho is, running right down the middle of Kuhio Street that way.

You've been spotted. Deep safety and a lineman. Take 'em out quick. The rest of the defense is less than a block behind them.

He's been intercepted. Ho has been intercepted. That's Heinz, the deep safety, and Davis, a lineman. They have Ho trapped between them.

The lineman's only got a short club. Do the deep safety first.

And that's Davis getting in some fine short club work there, but Ho pays him no attention as he faces off against Heinz.

The deep safety comes off balance on a lunge. Catch his arm.

Ho's making his move. He's broken Heinz's arm! He's broken Heinz's arm.

Go to one knee and press the lineman.

Ho's down, he's up, he has Davis over his head. What a slam!

The goalyard tender's standing too far back. A running butt'll take you across.

There's a running butt, and TOUCHDOWN!

Good work, buddy. You listen real good. You keep on working with me as well as that, and you're gonna live to a ripe old age.

Tuesday, July 13, 2010

From the window of his Russian Hill apartment, T.K. idly contemplates the continual stream of monstrous air-cushioned freighters whooshing in and out of San Francisco Bay. Fully nine out of ten are painted with the gray and white piping that signifies ownership by one of the Asian nations, Japan, Vietnam, Korea, Thailand, banded together to form the world's most progressive and powerful industrial cartel. T.K. considers the ships a nice contrast to the dark green of the bay, an observation which fairly well sums up his disinterest in the whole area of world politics and economics.

Today is Tuesday, his favorite day of the week. The pain and fatigue taper off on Monday. Wednesday and Thursday are practice days, scrimmages and theory sessions eat them up. Friday is traveling day or, if the game is being played in San Francisco, the day he and Coach Carrerra select the playing area. Saturday he scouts the street, and he rests. Then, of course, there's Sunday.

T.K. usually spends his Tuesdays in bed with some willing young lady. Unfortunately, this Tuesday's young lady has literary rather than romantic collaboration in mind.

For the past few months, Sarah Lauffler has accompanied T.K. everywhere, to practices, to other cities, to bars, to chalk talks. To hospitals. She's watched him play in and win eleven games.

Now she sits cross-legged on the floor with a massive sheaf of papers beside her.

"This is a final draft of my article," she explains. "What I'd like you to do is to read what I've put together to make sure I have all my facts straight."

He accepts the manuscript and carries it to his favorite chair, a mock-leather recliner. He flips on the overhead pin-light and begins to read.

Considering its eventual destination, the article's balanced, almost flattering tone surprises him.

"You're really going to run this in *EBS?*" he asks when he's finished.

"Yes. I think the story makes an interesting point, one that *EBS* too often overlooks, namely, that football players are human beings, subject to the whole range of human emotion, to pride, to love and even sometimes to compassion."

"That's all so much chic journalistic bullshit." He waves her manuscript at her. "You completely overlooked the whole reason I play football. For the money. To support myself in the style to which I've grown accustomed."

Vigorously she shakes her head. "It doesn't add up. Even given your high style, you still make twice as much money as you openly spend."

"I save a lot."

Again, the headshake. "Your bank account shows a balance of a little more than two hundred dollars."

"*EBS* writers are a very sneaky bunch."

"And very thorough. Granted, you may be in it for the money, but if so, where does that money go?"

T.K. gets up and walks to the window. Off in the distance he can make out the hills of Marin and, beyond that, the blue, unsullied sky.

He turns decisively to face her. "I'll show you."

They catch a pedicab to the commuter station. There they board a steam tram heading south. They leave San Francisco, traveling past San-Alto-Jose along the elevated tracks above the bay. They cut inland at South Point, switch trams at Gilroy, head through Hollister and finally get off in Los Banos. The whole trip takes just under an hour.

They rent two bicycles from the Hertz desk in the tram depot, and pedal off along Kings Road Canal almost to Dos Palos. There T.K. pulls up outside a large white house, a Victorian confection, all steeples and intricate carvings and stained-glass windows. The house is in excellent repair, obviously the end result of someone's laborious care. The area around the house is quite different, however. The ground is hard-packed and dry. Although it's been cultivated and planted, nothing grows on it. As the wind comes up, a cloud of dust blows off, enveloping the bottom of the house, giving it the appearance of a sugar cake rising up out of a smoky caldron of desolation.

With Sarah standing beside him, T.K. knocks on the door.

A frail, bald-headed man answers. "My God, can it be? T.K.," he cries out. "What a nice surprise. You were just here. We didn't expect you back again for another month. Ma, come see who's here. It's T.K." A buxom, white-haired old lady rushes forth from the kitchen. She engulfs T.K. in a clasping embrace.

"Sarah," says T.K., disentangling himself, "I'd like you to meet Frieda and Tanner Shaw."

"How do you do," Sarah says.

"Come in, come in," says Frieda.

"In a minute," T.K. responds. "First, I'd like to show Sarah the shed."

Tanner fetches a brightly polished key and gives it to T.K.

T.K. and Sarah head off toward a large metal shed out back, an incongruous entity contrasted with the picture postcard charm of the house proper.

"Who are they?" Sarah asks.

"They were my parents' best friends. They lived on the farm next to ours." T.K. points off into the distance. "If you squint, you can see an electrified boundary out there. Everything on the other side of that boundary belongs to the government. The Shaws' farm is out there in the middle of it somewhere." He turns to stare at her, angry, not with her but with the amorphous robber baron named bureaucracy. "When the Shaws lost their farm to the government, they moved in here. But the government siphons off all their water for its crops, leaving the Shaws with nothing but a lump of dust. Oh, they try to make their new land as good as their old. They nurture it, they tend it, they try to make it live. It repays them by blowing away." Another cloud of dust billows by.

He inserts the key in a big chrome lock, twists the lock free and opens the door.

Inside is an object covered with a large gray tarp. T.K. pulls off the tarp to expose a sleek red car underneath.

"It's very nice," Sarah says, trying without much success to keep the disappointment out of her voice. She had expected

T.K.'s secret expense to be somewhat more exotic than a car. "It's in museum-quality condition."

"See that storage tank in the corner. I keep it filled with gasoline. Six gallons. Costs me almost as much to fill that tank as it did to buy the car in the first place. If I wanted to, I could drive this car right now, right out of here, right down the road and away."

"If the environmental agencies would give you a permit, that is."

"You're so practical. Here, slide in." He opens the passenger door. "I never worry about a permit out here. I grease the local sheriff, bribe a nosy neighbor or two, and away I go, the first Tuesday of every month. Next time I take it out, you're more than welcome to ride along."

"What kind of a car is this?" she inquires.

"It's called a Porsche. This model is a 911T. It has six horizontally opposed cylinders, all covered with light alloy cylinder heads. It has V-patterned overhead valves and a forged eight-main-bearing crankshaft. Its SAE net horsepower rating is 129. It was probably the most efficient sports car ever built."

Sarah plainly doesn't understand any of it. "So this is where all your money goes. On running this car."

"A good percentage of it, yes, but not all." T.K. slips behind the wheel. "My folks lived about seventy miles from here. Just outside the town of Armona. We rented our farm from a wealthy family in Sacramento until we finally scraped up enough to buy it outright. I grew up on it. I was born on that farm. Within two weeks of each other, my mother and father died there. They're both buried out back of the farmhouse, under an old fir tree. I was in my first season with the Prospectors when it happened. First they died, then not a month later the government started up its agricultural combine and confiscated my farm and my parents' graves along with it. I nearly went crazy. I hired teams of lawyers, poured ungodly sums of money into stopping it. Oh, the government offered to pay for having my parents disinterred and transferred to a cemetery of my choice, but that circumvented the whole point. There's a special, unbreakable bond that grows up between farmers and their piece of the earth. My folks' land was precious to them. I was determined to find a way they could stay on it. Eventually, I negotiated a compromise. The two hundred acres around the farmhouse was forfeit. I couldn't change that. But my lawyers found a way of forcing the government to give me the option of leasing the house and immediate grounds. Of course, the government put the rental fee at what it considered to be a prohibitively high level. It was a real dilemma for me. I had seriously been considering quitting football. I didn't like the brutality, I especially didn't like the killing. But football was the only way I could make enough money to afford to lease that house. So I made my choice. Now I devote almost half of my income to it. Ironic, isn't it? I bust my butt to lease something I can't even get to. The government doesn't let anybody travel through their agricultural empire, you know. Afraid someone might trample a cornstalk or crush a soybean. But I know the house, the fir tree, the graves. I know they're out there."

He hunches across the steering wheel, peering down over the hood and out the shed door. Abruptly he straightens up. "It's not much of an accomplishment for twelve years of getting my brains beaten out, is it?"

Gently, understandingly, she touches his forearm. "It's something you had to do, and you did it with honor. There's nothing disgraceful in that. And, if you really want to, you're still young enough to start a new career."

"There's damned little market in industry for a professional savage."

"Surely you can do something."

"Not and earn this kind of money, I can't."

"Have you ever tried looking? Honestly, now."

He has to tell her the truth. "No."

"Then maybe, subconsciously, you like playing football more than you're willing to admit. Maybe it's really a form of sublimation for you, a means of proving your masculinity beyond the shadow of a doubt."

"Don't give me that cut-rate psychoanalytic crap. Don't peek inside my head. If I could get out of football, I would. It's a murderous business, and there's nothing good about dying."

"Oh, but there is. It releases you from all your obligations. Dead men don't have to keep up appearances."

"Let's just drop this whole thing right here, huh?" He chops his hand down, symbolically cutting off her assault on his motivations, and, simultaneously, stemming the rise of his temper. "And I didn't tell you all this for publication. I told it to you as a friend. Agreed?"

She nods her head.

"Good." In the time it takes him to climb out of the car, he shakes the venomous residue of his outburst completely out of his system. It's the mark of a pro. "Let's go inside," he suggests jovially. "The Shaws probably will ask us to dinner, and I can personally attest to the mouth-watering experience that would be."

Sarah gets out of the car. They lock up the shed and, together, head for the house.

Wednesday, July 14, 2010

"Finding out what you wanted to know was so childishly easy," Sarah says into the vid-phone, "I almost feel you're entitled to a partial refund."

"Apply it toward the next aspect of your assignment," says her employer. "We're no longer thinking in terms of contingencies. We have a specific use for T.K. Mann. I want you to continue to see him. Tell him you're expanding your article into a six-part series. Gain his confidence. His intimate confidence. I don't believe I need go into explicit detail."

"Not so long as you keep sending money."

The senator laughs. "You're an unprincipled bitch, Sarah."

"In my business, that's what it takes to survive."

"We have a great deal in common, my dear, a great deal indeed." Chuckling, he breaks the connection.

SUPERBOWL XXI, THE GAME

Saturday, January 1, 2011, 12:55 A.M.

The Prospectors take the kickoff deep on Myrtle. The Minutemen, bolstered by an advantage in manpower, smother the return at Grove.

For his first call of the game, T.K. puts Frazier on the line at right tackle to compensate for the loss of Minick and Healy, and sends Howe in motion to the right. He gives to Clausen, who swings around right end. The Minutemen smear Clausen for no gain.

On his way to the huddle, T.K. notes the defense. A standard 5-4-2. Matision has shifted himself to free safety, and is juking the line. Bumbo Johnson, back in the middle linebacker slot, swings his short club menacingly. Just at the sight of it, T.K.'s kidneys start to throb.

The situation calls for a stall. A team can operate moderately well down one man. But not down two. The Prospectors need to buy some time to give Healy a chance to recover. To do it, the ball carrier has to shake his pursuit and stay out of sight for as long as possible. Naturally, he has to keep moving forward or the referees will call a deliberate stalling penalty, but he needn't move forward very fast.

The Prospectors huddle up.

"Clausen, replace Frazier at right tackle," T.K. commands. "We'll run a blue series forty left." This means the fullback, Frazier, will take the ball on a slant across left tackle. The left tackle and guard will cross block to open the hole. "Once you're in the clear, cut into that movie hall across the street. It's an old son of a bitch, and it still has a stage with a place out in front for a band. Shag your ass down into that band place. There's a door there that leads under the stage. From there you come out in an alley. I want everybody else to go left around the movie. Frazier, you head right when you get to the alley. There's a bakery or something next door. Go through it and come back out here to Grove. With any luck, there won't be anybody waiting to meet you. After that, you're on your own. Play it loose, but play it slow. We need maybe another hour to get Healy back in the game. Got it?"

Frazier nods.

"Everybody clear?"

A series of affirmative grunts.

"O.K. On two."

The Prospectors line up.

"Hut one," barks T.K., "hut two."

Brye, filling in at center, sends the ball spiraling back. T.K. hands off to Frazier only seconds before Bumbo Johnson engulfs him. T.K. wrestles Johnson clear and breaks away.

The play goes well. Frazier bulls his way into the theater. Dedemus and DeGeller trap his pursuit in the lobby. The other Prospectors pull out of contact and head off to the left around the movie. As T.K. hoped, the Minutemen follow.

T.K. runs with the pack. They reach the back of the movie and shag left, opposite the direction taken by Frazier. Assuming the Prospectors are on their way to give their ball carrier blocking support, the Minutemen follow closely behind.

The whole play is working like a charm. By now Frazier must certainly be vanished and gone.

Then T.K. hears the depressing sound of an amplified whistle coming from Grove.

Numbly he returns to the line of scrimmage, knowing full well what he'll find there.

As he suspected, Orval Frazier is down on the street. Judging from the cockeyed angle of his arm, it appears to be broken.

It also comes as no surprise to T.K. to see Harv Matision standing over Frazier.

Grinning sadistically.

Yes, it's going to be a very rough day indeed.

AP NEWS SERVICE—FOOTBALL ROUNDUP—MONDAY, JULY 19, 2010—SUNDAY'S ROUND OF FOOTBALL ACTION PRODUCED A MAJOR UPSET AS THE MOBILE GREYS RUINED THE PROSPECTORS' UN-BLEMISHED RECORD DEFEATING THE SAN FRANCISCO BALL CLUB 98 TO 66. QUARTERBACK T.K. MANN, INJURED EARLY IN THE GAME, SPENT THE ENTIRE FIRST HALF RED-CROSSED. HE CAME BACK IN THE SECOND HALF, BUT NEVER REGAINED HIS COMPOSURE. TEAM OFFI-CIALS REFUSE TO COMMENT ON THE EXTENT OF HIS INJURIES. THE LOSS OF MANN AT THIS PARTICULAR POINT IN THE SEASON COULD PROVE A DISTINCT SETBACK TO THE PROSPECTORS' SUPERBOWL HOPES, ESPECIALLY SINCE NEXT SUNDAY THE PROSPECTORS COME UP AGAINST THE STILL UNDEFEATED NEW ENGLAND MINUTEMEN, WHO YESTERDAY COASTED TO AN EASY 102 TO 60 VICTORY OVER THE HAPLESS JUNEAU MIDNIGHTS. THE WIN RUNS THE MINUTEMEN'S UNBROKEN STRING OF VICTORIES TO 48, ONLY ONE SHY OF THE LEAGUE RECORD. PLAYING HIS USUAL FREE-WHEELING GAME, HARV MATISION CARRIED FOR 300 YARDS. HE ALSO DISPATCHED TWO MID-NIGHT PLAYERS, INCLUDING POPULAR VETERAN DURKIE BROWN.

SUPERBOWL XXI, THE GAME

Saturday, January 1, 2011, 1:15 A.M.

With stunning accuracy, T.K. bores in two short passes to make the first down.

Noticeably bowlegged but at least ambulatory, Healy comes back into the game. Frazier, his arm encased in a rigid vinyl splint, comes back in, too. It isn't the first time he's played with a portion of his body shattered, nor, probably, will it be the last. T.K. puts him at tackle, moves Pfleg over to fullback.

On the second play of the next series, Lammy Howe catches the Minutemen's left tackle with a vicious forearm. The tackle winds up on the street, his body spread-eagled on the sidewalk, his neck hanging over the curb. His protective Plexiglas mask has popped open. Howe takes advantage of it by kicking him hard in the face. When the Minutemen's mediman pulls the tackle's helmet off, he's got blood running out of his ears. He's sure to be out for the game.

Howe's evened the odds. In appreciation, T.K. gives him a hearty slap on the butt.

No longer outnumbered, T.K. is able to take the Prospectors on a long drive, down Phillips to Irving. They fight in one end of a vacant lot and out the other, battle through several buildings to emerge on Temple. From there, the goalyard is just down the street at the corner of Temple and Dern.

T.K. keeps the snap and dashes into a department store. He takes the steps to the second floor two at a time. He finds himself in the ladies' department. Pausing for a moment to get his bearings, he spots the fire escape and heads toward it. He almost reaches it, when someone tackles him from behind. He hits, rolls and comes up in his defensive stance, the ball tucked into the gut pocket in his jersey, his right arm, fingers extended, thumb folded under, half cocked at the elbow, his left arm straight out in front of him.

He's facing Harv Matision.

"Say your prayers, old man," spits Matision, the store lights gleaming off his long knife. Matision lunges.

T.K. parries with his left arm, forcing the knife up and away while at the same time hooking his left leg behind Matision's left knee. He pushes backwards and the younger man goes down. T.K. shoves the first items he can lay his hands on, a pile of lingerie, on Matision to tangle him up and impede him, then, again, makes for the fire escape. But Matision, quicker to recover than T.K. anticipates, catches his legs and drags T.K. down. T.K. rolls over, his first thought for the knife. He kicks at it feebly, but catches it perfectly, knocking it out of Matision's hand. It goes chattering across the floor and comes to rest under a counter.

Matision scrambles for it, but T.K. hangs on to his legs, dragging him down.

Just when it looks like a standoff, Matision squirms free, stands, tugs at a large display case nearby filled with jewelry, and topples it over on T.K.'s body. T.K. sees it coming, but can't get out of the way in time. Its entire weight comes down on him. Try as he might, he can't move.

The referee blows his whistle.

After extricating T.K., the referee places down a red marker. Tomorrow, a joint Minutemen/Prospectors restitution squad will come here and reimburse the store's owner for damages. The referee then moves the ball out to the street, placing it at a point approximately the same distance from the goalyard as it had been inside.

Two plays later, literally within spitting distance of the goalyard, on a straight power push, T.K. fumbles the ball.

Matision scoops it up. On the very next play, in a brilliant display of evasive running, he streaks 600 yards for the touchdown.

He also runs in the extra point.

Score: Minutemen 14, Prospectors 0.

Dedemus and DeGeller both are knocked unconscious on the kickoff.

Zack Rauscher hustles out, pulling his white, roller-mounted medical box behind him. In it he has everything necessary to provide any medical aid short of major surgery. From a compartment underneath, he pulls out two cloth red crosses, which he lays over Dedemus and DeGeller. He opens the top of the box, pulls out two capsules of ammonia, snaps one open and waves it under Dedemus' nose. No response. He tries the same treatment on DeGeller with similarly negative results.

He gives T.K. the secret high sign, left hand, two fingers extended, to helmet. Out for at least one play, possibly the whole rest of the quarter. Both of them.

Unbidden, and definitely unwanted, a forebodingly gloomy sense of imminent defeat settles firmly over the Prospectors.

Television Program Ratings for the Week Ending July 16, 2010

Rank	Program	Rating	Network
1.	SFL Game of the Week	94.3	IBC
2.	Wednesday Night Football Highlights	90.7	IBC
3.	The Timothy Enge Show	86.2	IBC
4.	Thirteen to Twelve	86.0	IBC
5.	Deal Me In	72.1	ABS
6.	The Bully Boys	71.9	IBC
7.	Austin X	71.4	FBC
8.	Eagle Mirado	71.0	IBC
9.	Who's Got the Bibbles?	69.7	ABS
10.	Danny and Dee	67.5	ABS

Compiled by the A. C. Neilsen Rating Service, all rights reserved.

Thursday, July 22, 2010

The Timothy Enge Show opens, naturally enough, with a shot of Timothy Enge. He's seated in the midst of what appears to be a large, well-appointed den lined with rows of framed journalistic awards. In his lap is a brown clipboard, the source, as regular viewers are well aware, of his incisive, frequently embarrassing, oftentimes humorous, always interesting questions. From what can be seen of it when Timothy Enge tilts it provocatively toward the camera—the writing on its top sheet is crowded exceptionally close together—there'll be no idle banter tonight.

Timothy Enge begins his show. "This Sunday, ladies and gentlemen, the streets of San Francisco will resound to the primordial clash of giants in a contest which promises to be the most exciting football game of the season, perhaps the most exciting football game of *any* season." He speaks with the intrepid

self-reliance of a man well aware that of all Americans watching television at this very moment, better than 85 per cent have
chosen to watch him. "On the one hand, we have the San
Francisco Prospectors. Tied for first place in their conference,
they have to win to stay on top. On the other hand, the New
England Minutemen. Number one in their conference, un-
beaten in forty-eight games, only one victory shy of a new
league record. The Prospectors and the Minutemen. They're
playing their thirteenth game of the year this Sunday, and it's
going to be unlucky for somebody. But who? Let's see if we
can get a hint." He swivels his chair to one side.

"On my right, I have T.K. Mann, quarterback of the San
Francisco Prospectors, a well-respected and experienced professional who certainly needs no introduction." T.K. nods in the
direction of the camera. Actually, at this moment, he's nowhere
near Timothy Enge. Enge is in his New York studio, T.K. at his
San Francisco apartment. T.K. has no idea where Harv Matision, who is also on the show, is emanating from, most likely
somewhere in Boston. Camera trickery projects them hologramically into each other's presence, pulling the affair off so
successfully that T.K. would swear Enge and Matision are actually sitting only a matter of feet away from him in his own
living room. They're all three given representational access to
each other to facilitate correct bodily and facial reactions.
Home viewers see the three seated in Timothy Enge's den.

Enge swivels left. "And on my left, the one they call elec-
trifying, the one they call stupendous, the one they call the
most promising football player of all time. I give you the one
they call Harv Matision."

Matision, slouched in his chair, flips his hand disdainfully
out at the viewers, middle finger extended. "Eat shit," he says,
hauling out one of the profane openings that is as much his
trademark as his chilling insolence.

"Possibly there's a complete recluse off someplace who has
never heard of Harv Matision," Enge continues. "For the
benefit of that unfortunate and provincial nonentity, let me
describe him. Harv Matision. He's twenty-four years old. He

learned to play football in the Boston streets. He won the Silver Star for heroism in the Brazilian War. He started out his professional football career as a hidden safety, in that capacity setting three consecutive league kill records. In his first season as a quarterback, he led his team not only to an undefeated season, but also to a victory in Superbowl XX. He was last year's unanimous choice for player of the year. Harv"—he puts his hand on Matision's arm—"welcome to the show."

"Yeah," mumbles Matision, clearly bored.

"Harv," says Enge in the mock serious way that tells his viewers he's only joking, "let me ask something of you. There's a story, possibly apocryphal, going around that when you were a child, you were so tough that whenever you needed money you would pull out one of your teeth and leave it under your pillow. Is there any truth to that anecdote?"

Matision comes as close as he can to a chuckle. It rumbles forth sounding somewhat like a cross between a belch and a coyote's howl. "No, that ain't true. It was my baby sister's teeth I pulled out. No sense letting all those good teeth go to waste, I figured. Hell, she's gonna lose 'em anyway. Kids always do, you know."

Enge laughs, slapping his chair in delight, and turns to T.K. He consults his clipboard. "T.K., you were injured in last Sunday's game with the Greys. Are you well enough to play in this crucial contest on Sunday, or will the Prospectors have to rely on some other knight in shining armor to lead them on in their charge against the seemingly impregnable fortress that is Harv Matision and the New England Minutemen?"

The truth is, T.K. has three shattered ribs. Every movement is sheer agony for him. Even sitting here quietly in his own living room gives him pain. He's undergoing extensive bone-reknitting therapy at Stanford, but even the fine doctors at Stanford can't perform miracles. He'll be only 80 per cent recovered by Sunday. He answers the question. "I had some minor injuries—a dislocated arm and a slipped disk." They are two very common, and very easily correctable, football injuries. T.K. has never had either. "I'll be as good as new by Sunday." Wearing a special brace, he is going to play in the game.

"Well, that's certainly good news for Prospector fans," says Timothy Enge. "Tell us, T.K., without giving out any sensitive secrets, what will be your game plan for this critical encounter?"

"Well, Timothy, I plan to rely on the fundamentals. Running, blocking, passing, defense and conditioning. I think we've got the best team in the league. This Sunday, I hope to prove it."

"A commendable aspiration, T.K., one which I am sure you will do your utmost to achieve." He swings around toward Matision. "Harv, you've heard your opponent. Tell me, what does your game plan call for?"

Matision stares straight ahead at the camera. When he speaks, his voice has a menacing growl to it, the snarl of a caged meat eater, overlooked at feeding time. "I only got one game plan. It's the same for every game I'm in. I do my best to kill every fucking ball carrier I get my hands on."

"I see," says Timothy Enge. "So you're going to rely on weaponry to bring about an attrition of the opposition."

"Shit," clarifies Matision, "I'm gonna use my knife to kill Prospectors. And I'm gonna start with Mr. T.K. Mann."

T.K. halfway bolts out of his chair, but a burst of pain forces him to sit back down.

Matision goes on. "I'm better than T.K. Mann ever was. I'm better now than he ever will be. Just so there's no doubt, I'm gonna slit his throat on national TV." Matision pulls out a knife.

My God, thinks T.K., I'll bet he takes it to bed with him.

Flipping his wrist, Matision opens it. "For you folks at home, here's a little sampler of what you're gonna see." Abruptly, he lunges for T.K.'s throat.

Completely unprepared for such an action, T.K. reacts by rolling sideways, but the pain of doing so throws him off balance. Instead of clearing the chair, he hits its arm, flops ungracefully over, and, chair and all, falls to his apartment floor with a dull thud. Matision stands over him laughing. From the floor, T.K. swings at him, barely able to see through tears of pain, but, of course, since Matision is only hologramically present, he doesn't connect. His swing, as altered by the camera's angle, appears to miss Matision by six inches. The two are abruptly frozen, T.K. lying on the floor, Matision towering over him in laughter.

The scene cuts to a close-up of Timothy Enge. "As you have just seen for yourselves, ladies and gentlemen, nerves are stretched to the breaking point for this game. This was only the beginning. I urge you to tune in to most of these same stations this coming Sunday to see the end."

The scene fades to black.

Friday, July 23, 2010

"You handled the Enge show nicely," Pierce Spencer tells Ida Moulay. He flips off his videoscope and pops out the tape. "I liked it. It fostered just the right degree of controversy. We'll have every set in the country tuned in on Sunday. Mann reacted exactly as I thought he would." He returns the tape to a round fist-sized storage box. "How long did it take you to teach Matision his lines?"

Ida smiles guilefully. "Oh, not long at all. You see, I didn't have to. I sat in the control booth myself and fed them to him personally. I thought we might as well get some extra mileage out of that implanted receiver in his head. We certainly spent enough money putting it there."

Spencer regards her with approval. "That's the way to take charge, Ida."

She flushes. It's nothing less than Spencer's highest accolade. "Tell me," she asks, "who's going to win? Mann or Matision?"

"I don't know," he answers soberly. "I haven't quite decided yet. If only I could come up with some way whereby they would both win. Not a tie, I don't mean that. What I mean is a clear-cut victory for both. It would be a natural for a rematch in the Superbowl. Perhaps Mann wins the game, but Matision . . . Matision what?" Then it comes to him. "Of course. Ida, get me the media file on that Prospector player. Mann's friend. What's his name? Yes, Eddie Hougart."

SUPERBOWL XXI, THE GAME

Saturday, January 1, 2011, 4:45 A.M.

Shadows that metamorphose into hulking linemen, a noise off behind, footsteps in the blackness, everyplace to hide, the terror of blindness, the chill of obscurity, this is the night shroud of football.

The Minutemen's game has been falling steadily apart ever since they scored their second touchdown. They're having trouble putting everything together the way they did earlier. They aren't able to rack up yardage any more, to inflict injuries, or to lose their pursuit. The game went too easily for them in the opening minutes. They became overconfident.

The Prospectors, on the other hand, have come very much alive thanks to a stiffening run of good luck. Dedemus and DeGeller both came back into the game after missing only two plays. D'Armato sliced a Minutemen ball carrier's knee ligament, putting him permanently out of the game and giving the Prospectors a one-man edge.

T.K. has used the imbalance to good advantage. On almost every play he sends his extra man downfield. If the Minutemen pull a man out of the line to cover, T.K. then scrambles on the ground. If they don't cover, if they blitz, he passes.

The technique has worked consistently well, so well that the Prospectors are now within sixty-five yards of the Minutemen's goalyard. They have three downs in which to make it.

"I got the middle linebacker's number, T.K.," says Frazier in the huddle. "I can twist that Johnson dude around my little finger." He shakes the temporary cast Rauscher has slapped on his broken arm. "I got him coming, I got him going. You put it right over him, and I'll see he ain't there to stop it."

"T.K. nods his recognition of Frazier's suggestion. "Lammy," he asks, "how's your leg?"

Howe injured it three plays ago. He's been walking with a

limp ever since, but his running game doesn't seem to have suffered. "Feels O.K. I don't think I can handle many quick cuts, but I can carry straight ahead good enough."

"Super. It's gonna be a red series fifty-four." Howe will carry straight up the middle. "On two. Check with me at the line." This means T.K. reserves the right to change the play audibly once he's seen the defense.

The Prospectors break, and line up.

T.K. surveys the Minutemen's defense. They've got five men on the line, four back. Johnson at middle linebacker is riding it close in. Frazier can get to him easily. The red fifty-four should work. "On three." An odd number means the play called in the huddle is go. "Forty-four, thirteen, twenty-six, hut one, hut two."

He fakes a hand-off to Clausen, lays the ball gently into Howe's gut, and steps back to fake the pass. Frazier pops the linebacker a good one. Howe steps into the hole and is gone. He makes it nearly ten yards before a safety brings him down with a bola.

"Let's try it again," says T.K. in the huddle. "Check with me at the line. On one."

Johnson didn't learn his lesson. He's playing it exactly the same as before.

"On one. Sixty-five, ninety-seven, thirty-two, hut one."

Again, Howe bursts through the hole. This time, he darts into an alleyway off Temple and disappears. The Minutemen team gives chase.

T.K. lets them go. He's got a lot of confidence in Howe's ability to break away, so T.K. heads directly for the goalyard. When he arrives, there are no less than three Minutemen there ahead of him. Obviously, the Minutemen know something about Howe's abilities, too. T.K. hides, pressing himself into a doorway, one with a good view of the goalyard, and waits for Howe to arrive.

Almost from out of nowhere, Howe does. Completely ignoring the three-to-one odds against him, he steams full bore for the goalyard. T.K. bolts from the doorway and sprints for the goalyard, too, heading toward it at a ninety-degree angle from Howe. By a very slight margin, T.K. will reach the goalyard first. It's a play the Prospectors have worked on again and again.

Two of the Minutemen, knives drawn and ready, brace themselves to face Howe; after all, he, being the ball carrier, is the more important of the two. The remaining Minuteman, a short club in his hand, prepares himself to stop T.K.

At the last instant, T.K. cuts in front of Howe and throws himself cross body at the two knife-wielding Minutemen. Taken by surprise, the two of them topple sideways, clearing a tiny entryway to the goalyard. Howe hits it, but the third Minuteman manages to catch a shoulder in his stomach, so he doesn't make it across. Howe backs off for another try. He charges ahead. A jumbled mass of arms reach out to stop him. Suddenly he freezes, jerks bolt upright. Ribbons of red pour out of his chin. He yanks out the long knife imbedded there. It's his last living action, and the first death of the game.

A whistle blows, ending the quarter.

Score: Minutemen 14, Prospectors 0.

The Question Man

Senator Cy Abelman (D-Oregon) recently proposed a bill that would eliminate the use of knives, clubs and rifles from the game of football and would at the same time limit the length of play to twelve hours. What's your opinion?

That's the trouble with these guys in Washington. Ain't none of 'em give a damn for the working stiff. Hell, I put in a hard four days at work, I look forward to watching football on Sunday. It's the best relaxation there is. You take out the weapons, you shorten the playing time, you rip the guts out of the game. All my buddies, was you to ask 'em, would tell you the same.

Tuli Jones, Automated Construction Crew Monitor

If you want to know what I think, I think they oughta pass a law giving every player a gun. Wouldn't that be something!
Mose Stern, Bicycle Mechanic

Cut it shorter? Not on your life. Even when there's nothing much going on, when a guy's hiding out, for instance, is O.K. by me. It's sort of spooky, you see, waiting for something to happen, waiting for somebody to get caught, for some guy to get his. No, I say we've got a good thing going. Let's leave it alone.
Hense Taglione, Apprentice Crystallographer

I like long games. I feel like I'm getting my money's worth in a long game. If Congress is going to do anything, they should make the games even longer. Maybe put in another quarter. And while they're at it, I think giving the hidden safety another couple of bullets like that Senator Barin [R-New Jersey] wants to do is a damn good idea. It would make for more suspense, if you know what I mean.
Tedson Lehman, Househusband

I don't understand who he's trying to protect? Those athletes know what they're getting into when they go out there. They're getting paid big money for it. If they catch a hard one, well, that's breaks. Who am I to worry about them? Do they worry about me?
Alberta Prouliere, Clerk/Transcriber

(On July 24, 2010, the preceding column, syndicated by the American Feature Service, a subsidiary of IBC, appeared in the Saturday supplements of 412 newspapers.)

Saturday, July 24, and Sunday, July 25, 2010

The television control room for the Prospectors-Minutemen game is located inside a mobile trailer parked at the intersection of Lombard and Stockton. The trailer itself is a stark, drab, lifeless gray vehicle, completely devoid of ornamentation or color of any sort. That's outside. The inside of the trailer is an entirely different matter. Inside burn a seemingly infinite collection of lights indicating the functioning state of the limbs, tendrils and organs that compose the giant named Entertainment. Is the giant moving too fast? A light flashes. Is it healthy? A light shines clear. Is a part of it diseased? A light flickers and dies. The lights are everywhere. Camera lights, sound intensity lights, voltage lights, elapsed playing time indication lights, time zone monitor lights, down status lights, scoring lights, lights of all hues, blinking on and off like a Christmas tree gone berserk.

In the midst of all these lights sits their omnipotent master, the program co-ordinator. At his discretion, a flicker will become a glow; a glow, a ring of blackness.

He sits before a master console filled with forty-nine tiny viewscreens, one for each cameraman covering the game both on the street and in the studio.

The flavor of the game and the clarity of its progress as it appears on home viewing screens is a result, solely, of the program co-ordinator's skill at the console—how cunningly he anticipates evasive actions, how quickly he sizes up the flow of power, how well he positions his cameramen relative to the players, from what angles he covers the letting of blood.

When the two teams, the Prospectors and the Minutemen, and their attendant cameramen come out onto the street, a series of blips will appear on a large screen in the center of the console. The blips indicate the location by number of every player on both teams, as well as the location of every cameraman. The players' jerseys and the cameramen's coveralls are woven from special radio frequency-sensitive material, each man being assigned his own discrete frequency. A sensor in the control room locks to each signal and feeds its position to a central computer which translates it into a cogent visual display of location.

The program co-ordinator wears an ear mike so that, using his cameramen's microphones, he can listen in on the quarterback's calls in the huddle and to the defensive calls at the line. On the basis of that information, and his own intuitive feel for the relative performances of the two teams, he issues instructions to his cameramen, notifying them what to look for and which way to shoot. If he's careless, if he re-positions his cameramen too obviously or too soon, he can inadvertently affect the game's fairness by tipping the defense, most of whom are cagey enough to give the cameramen at least a casual glance before the snap to see how they're set up to cover the play.

After the snap, the program co-ordinator has to react at least as quickly as the players he's covering, relaying directions and pulling his cameramen into proper position, all the while remaining flexible enough to shift his coverage away from the ball carrier and to a more interesting or violent confrontation occurring elsewhere on the street.

A backup man stands behind the program co-ordinator at all times, ready to take over at a moment's notice should the PCO suffer a nervous collapse brought on by exhaustion, something which happens all too frequently in the heat of a game.

The program co-ordinator, like his cameramen, works only one quarter of the game.

On a raised platform immediately behind the program co-ordinator, in a glassed-in, soundproofed booth of his own, sits Timothy Enge. He has one giant screen showing him what the people at home are seeing. By looking out into the main control room, he can see the program co-ordinator's master console, as well. Near his right hand is a computer terminal ready to call up all manner of football facts and figures. At his left hand, concealed behind the arm of his chair, he has a food and drug dispenser. More than the food, he needs the drugs, mainly to stay awake, since he will work the game's entire twenty-four hours. There's a cameraman just to his right and in front of him, a makeup man just to his left and out of camera range in back.

The two teams come out onto the street.

Everything's perfect.

The program co-ordinator's lights radiate with a satisfying luster.

Timothy Enge is in excellent voice.

The Prospectors and the Minutemen line up at the intersection of Third and Market.

At precisely twelve midnight, the Minutemen kick off, and the game begins.

There is no threat of boredom in the control room today. The game turns into one of the hardest-fought battles of the year. The lead changes hands five times in the first three quarters, and the blood flows freely. Harv Matision is penalized four times for stabbing after the whistle. Once more and he'll be ejected from the game. Usually a free safety, he's shifted himself to middle linebacker for this game to give himself more of an opportunity to harass T.K. Mann. And he seems to be doing a fairly creditable job of it. T.K. is having to call up every reserve of strength he has to fend off Matision's wild, kamikaze attacks on him. T.K.'s been red-crossed six times for cuts—luckily for no more than one play each time—but his blood loss is reaching the point at which his mediman can't fortify him with rapid transfusions often enough to forestall a certain amount of weakening.

At the end of the third quarter, the Prospectors leave the street with a slim, two-point advantage.

While the cameramen do follow their charges into the locker room, the time-outs are covered in silence to prevent the two teams from inadvertently or purposefully listening in on each other's strategy discussions.

During this time-out, one control room monitor shows T.K. Mann lying prone on a training table. A trainer administers to him an injection of much needed coagulants and liquid nutriments. On another monitor, Eddie Hougart, Prospector halfback/deep safety, snoozes. On another, Bumbo Johnson, Minutemen halfback/deep safety, does push-ups to keep from stiffening.

But the viewers at home see Harv Matision. He's slumped in front of his locker. His left arm is bare, the protective pads have been removed. There's a piece of rubber tubing tied around his bulging left bicep. In his right hand, he balances a hypodermic needle. He holds it up between him and the camera, pushes the plunger, watches a thin stream of clear liquid shoot out. Searching with his index finger, he finds the big vein in the crook of his inner elbow, massages it several times to bring it into better view, and jabs the needle home. Keeping his thumb across the plunger, he unloosens the tubing by jerking it free with his teeth. The camera zooms in for a close-up of blood mixing with the needle's contents before it disappears into his arm, and from there pans up to his face, a portrait of relaxation and rapture.

Matision's hand flops down to his side. A trainer relieves him of the hypodermic. Actually, the trainer could just as easily have given him the shot, but Harv Matision puts a lot of stock in showmanship. Primarily, he's an exhibitionist, but he also knows that giving the public what it wants to see has a way of enlarging his paycheck. In fact, he'd undoubtedly consent to slice open his own wrists given enough monetary incentive and the promise of ample air time. He sits for a moment, quietly, stiffly, then jerks upward as if he's being lifted by some unseen string. His jerkiness doesn't last long, though. His motor functions quickly grow smooth, his motions burnish themselves to a slippery sheen. He becomes like a tornado, a human whirlwind, his movements almost too quick for the camera to follow. He slaps on his protective pads, takes some fast calisthenics to loosen himself up, and bolts for the locker room door.

The fourth quarter starts shortly thereafter.

The fourth quarter follows the pattern set by the first three. The Prospectors' hidden safety uses his bullet early on to keep a Minuteman from scoring. It's a perfect shot that catches the Minutemen's ball carrier squarely in the back of the knee, laming him instantly and giving the Prospectors a one-man advantage. The Minutemen retaliate swiftly, however, putting a Prospector permanently out of commission with a broken leg.

As time runs out, the Prospectors fight to hold onto their scant, two-point lead.

T.K. signals his referee. "Time hack," he calls out.

"Thirty-six minutes remaining in the game," the referee answers.

T.K. huddles his team around him. They're about in the center of the playing area. Mentally, T.K. checks off the important considerations. The Prospectors have suffered more physically than the Minutemen. Harv Matision's skills at last-minute scoring are almost the equal of T.K.'s own. T.K. weighs it out. He'd like to drive for the goalyard, rack up a security touchdown, take out some insurance, but to do so would be dangerous. The Minutemen's hidden safety still has his bullet and a long drive out in the open would give him too many chances to use it. T.K.'s not willing to trade men for points, so he decides on a time-eating stall. "Matision and his line have been putting the rush on me for the past four plays," T.K. says. "This time, I'm going to take advantage of it. We'll run a twenty-seven screen." A short pass to the center, Harland Minick. "And let's try and make this the last play of the game." Minick is one of the best hide-out men in the league. If anybody can buy them thirty-six minutes, he can. On this particular play, the line will let the defense through into the backfield. The pass will go over their heads to Minick, who should have plenty of room to run for cover. "On two."

They line up. T.K. checks the opposition. Standard ten-man scrimmage defense, a 5-3-2. He takes a quick look around at the street. A streetlight burns just behind him. The illumination is good, almost too good. If the defensive line doesn't take the fake, if one of them hangs back, Minick might have a tough time getting into the darkness.

"Hut one, hut two." Minick snaps the ball.

Something goes wrong! Matision doesn't blitz. He hangs back, as does the rest of his inner line.

His ends, though, come swooping down on T.K. like two avenging angels. T.K. backs off, five yards, and sets. He's totally exposed. Minick, his primary, is covered three ways. So are the guards, his two secondaries.

Then he sees Eddie Hougart completely open in the flat. At

the same time the first of the two ends reaches him, he lets the ball go in Eddie's direction.

It's a perfect, spiraling pass and it hits Hougart firmly at chest level, but it comes to him from out of the glare of the streetlight. Hougart grabs the ball, a reflex action, but his failing eyesight is filled with the streetlight's brilliance. He can't see to run. He hesitates for only an instant, but it's an instant too long.

Harv Matision is on him.

Hougart is a sitting duck. Matision could take him out easily with a casual overhip toss. Even an old-fashioned tackle would probably suffice. But Matision doesn't operate that way. To him, football is a game to be played for keeps, and that's just the way he plays it. For keeps.

Hougart doesn't see the knife, coming or going, either one. It's into his neck and gone passing through veins and muscle like an invisible steel ghost. He only realizes something is wrong when his neck starts to ache, and his throat fills with the sticky sweet wetness of blood. He falls to his knees, to his arms, to his back.

The whistle blows, ending the play.

T.K. gets up, and shakes himself off. He looks around to see what went wrong.

What he sees is his mediman laying a red cross over Eddie Hougart.

T.K. signals the mediman for a report. The mediman makes the dread two fingers down sign, team code for *dead man*. T.K. stares at him, unable to believe it. He signals the mediman for a repeat. Again he gets two fingers down in return.

Dumbly T.K. stumbles across the line of scrimmage toward where his friend lies. His referee blows his whistle. "Mann, back on sides, or I'll take the ball for a twenty-yard walk."

"Fuck you," responds T.K. under his breath. There are some things more important than twenty-yard penalties.

"O.K. If that's the way you want it," yells the referee. "Twenty yards. Stalling the game." He picks up the football and starts walking it off.

T.K. kneels beside Eddie. He's still alive, but only barely. The front of his uniform, his white home jersey, is a mottled maroon. His blue numerals are black where they've been drenched with his blood.

"T.K.," says Eddie, "T.K." His voice is a pleading burble, a gargle of supplication siphoned through agony.

"Right here, fellah. I got you. You're gonna be fine, just fine."

Eddie coughs up some bloody red spittle. "T.K.," he says quietly, almost peacefully. "How do you spell the fuck in meat?" It's Eddie's favorite exit routine. For him, it's the same as saying good-by.

"Eddie . . ." T.K. holds Eddie's head gently on his lap. "Eddie, no."

"Tell me, please, T.K., before it's too late." This time the peacefulness is replaced by teeth gritting to hold back a scream. "How do you spell the fuck in meat?" A great gob of phlegm spills out the corner of his mouth.

"There ain't no fuck in meat," T.K. whispers, his eyes misting over.

"Yeah, that's the same thing my butcher tells me," gasps Eddie. His laughter blends headlong into his death rattle.

The referee sets the ball down and blows his whistle.

Mechanically, T.K. stands and walks back to the line.

On the way, he passes Harv Matision. "And another candy-assed mother-fucker bites the dust," taunts Matision.

T.K. goes for him, wading in with hammering fists, but his overpowering shock and hatred make him careless. Matision manipulates him easily. He yanks T.K.'s arm back and around, separating it at the shoulder. Still, nearly fainting with pain, T.K. presses after him. It takes six referees to pull them apart.

As soon as the referees release him, T.K. heads, once again, for Matision, but he collapses before he can make two steps.

When he wakes up, the game is over.

The Prospectors have won it, 121 to 119.

They met one day
In the city by the bay.

The man they call Matision,
And the man they call T.K.
There was biting, there was fighting,
Was a lot of wrong and righting,
And two real angry heroes
When the smoke had cleared away.
Poor old Harv he lost the game,
T.K. Mann put him to shame,
Changed a winner to a loser nothing flat.
But when the game came to an end,
T.K. Mann had lost a friend,
And there can't be hardly nothing
Worse than that.
No, there can't be hardly nothing
Worse than that.
So they both got bones for picking,
Cause they each one took a licking,
Bound to be some blood spilled when they meet again.
Now, I know that ain't this year
But I'm gonna play the seer,
Say they'll both be back for XXI,
And only one will win.

(*The Ballad of T.K. and Harv*, written and sung by Timmy Longan and recorded on the PRIMO label, an IBC subsidiary. On Monday, July 26, 2010, it began the first of sixteen weeks on *Billboard*'s "Latest and First-ratest" listing.)

Monday, July 26, 2010

Every Monday after a home game, T.K. usually wakes up around noon, and heads for Tubber's Bar shortly thereafter. There's no entertainment at Tubber's, no food, no atmosphere, no loose women, nothing but liquor, that and a long-standing tradition of social privacy. Tubber's patrons, a motley collection of lower-middle-class working men, come there to forget about their jobs. They grant T.K. the same privilege. (Although, when back in the company of their non-Tubber's-frequenting cohorts, they're not above tossing out a casual reference to a Monday spent "drinking with the Mann," to lend extra credence to their knowledgeability about what went right—or wrong—with the Prospectors in their latest encounter.)

Usually, for T.K., Tubber's is a few brisk shots, an hour or two of exposure to humanity to transition himself back to a world where death doesn't wait around every corner, and off about his business.

Today, Tubber's is considerably more.

Tubber's waitress, Glenda, seeing T.K.'s glass is empty, rushes over with a refill: scotch, straight up. He's given her orders to keep a full glass in front of him for the rest of the afternoon.

"A victory celebration?" she asks.

"No, a wake," he snaps.

Glenda doesn't press him for details. When Tubber hired her, he gave her only two instructions. "Keep your hands out of the till," he told her, "and don't talk too much to the customers." Since Glenda was never much for idle conversation anyway, Tubber gets a 50 per cent compliance rate. In silence, she moves on to another table.

T.K. sits alone, his face to the wall. His right arm, the one Matision dislocated, is encased in an inflatable plastic sling. On the table in front of him there are two empty glasses lined up neatly side by side, perfectly squared off with the table's forward edge. "One dead Prospector," T.K. sings under his breath, "I'm so blue." It's a common rope-skipping chant, one that he hears children reciting a hundred times a day from the sidewalks outside his apartment. "Another gets his throat cut, and then there are two." He downs his scotch and positions the glass beside the others.

Glenda comes hustling over with his next one.

She sets it in front of him. He swishes it around a few times, and prepares to slug it down, when a hand touches his shoulder. He swings around. It's Sarah.

"I thought you might want some company."

On the one hand, it's the last thing in the world he wants. He's never considered mourning to be a team sport. Then again, he desperately needs to tell somebody about the deep, possibly irreparable fissure that Eddie's death puts into the fragile web of his self-esteem. He waves her to the chair next to him. "Drink?"

"No, nothing."

They sit in silence for several minutes, until, finally, T.K. speaks. "He died laughing, you know. He actually died laughing."

"I know. They showed it on television."

"Sometimes during a game I would find myself looking at him, thinking to myself, that old son of a bitch. Nobody's ever gonna get him. He's gonna be around forever. Only he turned out to be as mortal as everybody else. And there I am out there. Half a god. I can't give life, but I can sure as hell take it away."

"It wasn't your fault."

"But it was. It was my fault. I called a bad play. I've run it over and over a hundred times in my mind, and every time I come up with the same conclusion. I was under pressure. Two guys were coming after me. I was rushed. I threw to Eddie without really thinking. I should have realized the glare from the streetlight would blind him. I should have chalked the play off and eaten the ball. If I would have done that, Eddie would still be alive today." He tosses down his drink. Glenda appears with another.

"You can't expect to be able to account for every eventuality, every parameter, every variation of every parameter."

"Maybe that's my problem, then. You see, at one time, in my . . ." He stumbles over the words. ". . . In my younger days, I could."

She suspects he's bound and determined to spend the remainder of the day wallowing in self-doubt. "I don't know what else I can say."

"I don't think there's anything left. It might be better all around if I was by myself." He holds up his glass. "I'll see you later. Back at the apartment."

Silently she nods, gets up and leaves.

T.K. is about to down his drink when a man comes up to him. "You're T.K. Mann, aren't you." The man is quite out of place here. He's nattily dressed in a dark green striped jumpsuit. He wears an expensive necklace intricately fashioned out of silver and set with an authentic piece of wood. A double tam covers his head to both ears. But his most obvious incongruity is not in his apparel but in his complete disregard for proper etiquette, for the unwritten law of solitude to be followed here.

T.K. ignores him. "No autographs," he mumbles, turning all his attention to the glass in front of him.

The man shakes his head. "That's not why I'm here. I want to talk to you about yesterday's game."

T.K. has to strain to remain polite. He only partially succeeds. "Look, fellah. Some other time, O.K. I'm off duty right now."

"I think you'll change your mind when you hear what I have to say." He puts a card on the table, slides it over to a spot where T.K. can't help but read it. *Ebbet McKay,* it says, *Legal Staff, The Committee to End Blood Sports.* EBS! Damn. That Sarah. She must have brought him here.

T.K. flips the card to the edge of the table. "Look, Mr. McKay, just because I lost a good friend out there yesterday, that doesn't make me want to take up the crusade to chuck the whole game of football. So forget it."

McKay puts his hands on the rim of the table and leans in close. His voice carries a weighty, conspiratorial urgency. "Suppose I told you that your friend's killing was deliberately arranged. Not the specific details, mind you, but the fact that he would be killed was firmly determined at least five days prior to yesterday's game."

T.K. slams down his drink and turns angrily in the man's direction. "Come on. Cut the crap. Do you really expect me to believe that? That Eddie Hougart was set up? You're out of your mind. Who the hell could possibly set somebody up during a football game?"

"The International Broadcasting Company." McKay says it evenly, assuredly, giving it the confident inflection of truth.

"The television guys?"

"Precisely."

"But how? Why? And why Eddie?"

"IBC is promoting a grudge match between you and Harv Matision. They feel it will produce the biggest television audience of all time."

"Well, there I've got you. Now I know you're full of shit. I don't play Matision again this year. By the time we get together again, yesterday's game will be ancient history as far as the fans are concerned."

"Ah, but you're wrong, at least in one aspect of your reasoning. You are going to play Matision again this year."

"When?"

"In the Superbowl. In Superbowl XXI. You'll meet each other in Boston on January first."

"Come off it, will you? What are you, some kind of fortune-teller or something?" He pushes an empty glass McKay's way. "Here. Tell me more. Read the sludge in the bottom of this. Tell me I'm going to take an ocean voyage or kiss a stranger or inherit my old maiden aunt's French poodle."

McKay takes back his card. "I can't fully convince you here." He writes something on the reverse side of the card, and hands it back to T.K. "Come to this address. Tomorrow afternoon at three o'clock. I will show you evidence, hard, cold evidence, that I guarantee will leave you convinced."

"Yeah, well don't wait dinner for me if I don't show up."

"Mr. Mann, our philosophies may differ as to what constitutes a proper sport, but there's one factor I'm certain we would both acknowledge. Your friend was set up. His murder was arranged. And I think even you will agree that there's no sport in that." He leaves without waiting for a reply.

T.K. downs his drink. It burns all the way to his belly. He sets the glass on the table. Abstractly, he picks up the card. The address is in an excellent residential neighborhood out in the avenues.

Glenda brings him another drink. "Who was your friend?" she asks, not really caring.

"Just a fan," says T.K., jamming the card into his pocket. "Just a fan."

SUPERBOWL XXI, THE GAME

Saturday, January 1, 2011, 5:30 A.M.

The Prospectors' locker room at quarter time-out is a chaotic jumble of players, trainers and television cameramen. The players remain largely immobile, regaining strength, leaving it up to the others, the outsiders, to step over them or go around.

Trainers scurry about dispensing medication. Cameramen pursue better angles in their esthetic desire to capture it all artfully for posterity.

For those players who want food, a table off in one corner holds a varied supply, soymeat both cooked and raw, assorted vegetables, sugar cubes, chocolate bars, a basket of fruit disproportionately laden with oranges, an ice chest stocked with nutriment-enriched soft drinks, and an insulated jug of coffee.

The drug bin in the center of the room gets a much greater play, however.

Two of the Prospectors, Orval Frazier and Buddy Healy, undergo minor corrective surgery in the training room. After it's over, they'll be given rapid transfusions of plasma, coagulants and liquid nutriments to fortify them for the second quarter.

Harland Minick is carried off the field and taken to a hospital for extensive knee surgery.

Lammy Howe is carried off the field, too. After the game, when there is time for such things, there will be words of praise and tender sentiments for Lammy. For the time being, he's stuffed rather unceremoniously into a blue and gold body bag and stored in a deep freeze outside the locker room door. An ambulance from the mortuary specified in his player's file is already on its way over to pick him up.

T.K., as usual, bypasses drugs for food. He only nibbles, though, not wanting to risk cramping. He starts off with a fistful of raw cauliflower, follows that up with six ounces of broiled soymeat and grabs an orange for dessert. Digging a fingernail in on top, he peels it around in a circle, ending up with a continuous strip of peeling one inch wide and six inches long. Carefully, he breaks the orange into two hemispheres and pops one of them into his mouth. He chews it up and spits the seeds out into a corner.

While most quarterbacks have long turned to using chemicals or specially developed ointments on their hands to give them better ball control, T.K., as always, still swears by freshly squeezed orange juice. He rubs the remaining half of his orange between his two hands, squeezing the juice out over his palms and fingers. The juice contracts, dehydrates and tightens his skin and makes his hands sticky, exactly the way he likes them.

Coach Carrerra storms in. Actually, he spent the entire first quarter right here in the locker room watching the game. He left just prior to the team's arrival simply so he could come blustering back in with a proper showing of wrath. He's a great one for dramatic effect. He doesn't waste time on small talk.

"Brye," he says, his voice a husky condemnation. "Brye, that Minutemen tackle is making you look stupid out there. Stupid, do you hear me? Michalski. When the play is a break and run, you're supposed to break and run. How many times do I have to tell you? Leave your man alone. Break and run. DeGeller, the same goes for you. And D'Armato. Where the hell are you?" He makes a big point of searching out the hidden safety. "For Christ's sakes, when we've got a man on the goalyard, get down there on the street and put those knives of yours to work. I counted three separate times when you could have broken up a big gainer if you'd been on your toes."

D'Armato doesn't take kindly to criticism. He's seated on the

floor, his rifle propped up between his knees. He swings around
slightly so it's pointed, apparently by accident but pointed
nonetheless, directly at Coach Carrerra's belly. He fingers the
trigger. "Aw, fuck," he murmurs with the disdain a butcher
uses in declaring an animal unfit even to slaughter. He hops to
his feet, and goes to the drug bin. He props his rifle up on it,
and digs inside, pulling forth three green tablets. He swallows
one, and puts the other two inside his waistband for use during
the game.

"And T.K." It's a measure of how much Coach Carrerra
wants this one. He rarely, if ever, singles out his quarterback
for public censure. "On third and short yardage, they're stack-
ing on you. Anticipate it. Throw the bomb." To show his capacity for giving as well as taking away, he bestows a few plaudits,
as well. "Orval, good game. Don't let that cast hamper you. Use
it like a club. Swing it in there, man, swing it in there. Pfleg.
You're hitting real good. Keep it up."

Coach Carrerra walks to the blackboard and hastily sketches
a variation on the Prospectors' basic long-stem T offensive formation. All the while he's doing it, he keeps one eye warily on
the television set in the corner. It shows Timothy Enge super-
imposed on one of the game's early plays. The sound is turned
down, so there's no way to tell what he's saying. The set remains on so the Prospectors will know when they're being
shown here in the locker room. Granted, locker room scenes
are always broadcast silent, still, the wise exercise a modest
amount of caution whenever they see themselves on camera.
The use of lip readers is not unknown. And, of course, white
lines on a blackboard need no spoken commentary to explain
them. Should Coach Carrerra see himself appear on screen,
he'll flip the blackboard around to hide his diagrams.

"The first time we get our hands on the ball, let's try this
one." He draws a series of flowing patterns, white chalk dust
falling to the floor like seconds of life dropping away from the
men his lines represent. He's in the midst of drawing out his
second play when a referee knocks on the door.

"On the street, please. Five minutes remaining."

Reluctantly, T.K. stands. He pulls on his mesh gloves, drops his helmet into place and fastens his chin strap.

Carrerra puts down his chalk, and dusts off his hands. "Any last words, T.K.?"

For a moment, T.K. stands mute, glancing from one man to the other all around the room. "Let's tear ass," says T.K. softly, and charges through the door.

Yelling and screaming, his team follows hard in his footsteps.

The Vicarious Risk Factor in the Viewing of Televised Football: Its Relationship to Mental Health

An old and well-established tenet holds that individuals, to live a psychologically normal and meaningful existence, must participate regularly in some activity that provides an element of jeopardy. The rationale behind this is quite persuasive. Man evolved by successfully overcoming his natural risks. Risk helped to mold man's codes of honor, his pride, his loyalty. Studies also suggest risk helped prolong his youth and prowess, as well. In time, the old stimuli—the old dangers—were, for the most part, eliminated. But not the effect. Not the way man feels when confronted with risk or that man is still happiest when physically threatened. Risk is essential to man. A lack of it causes measurable permutations in his very makeup.

Unfortunately, in today's world, physically threatening activity is quite hard to arrange. Previous generations could envelop themselves in auto driving, horseback riding, hunting, airplane flying or the like. Today, of course, the shifting format of civilization has all but eliminated such activities. Yet man's need for exposure to risk still persists. The question is, how does modern man go about fulfilling that need?

The answer is ridiculously obvious. He does so vicariously by watching street football on television.

A frequently echoed condemnation of street football calls for an end to its viciousness. Many critics hold that the bloodshed and death have a morbidly counterproductive effect on the human psyche. I maintain to the contrary, however, that elim-

inating the threat of palpable censure from the game would
strip it of its foremost psychological emolument. Football fans
subconsciously view the game to experience the flavor of
danger, to receive an essential exposure to the risk they so desperately crave for their physical and mental well-being.

In this context, the end result of street football, brutality
included, is not only beneficial, but well-nigh a prerequisite to
heightened human functioning. Research affirms that man is
more efficient, more creative, longer-lived and more productive
as a result of risk. Preliminary evidence even indicates it may
appreciably improve his sex life. Man needs risk to function at
the height of his capabilities. Those who would remove the
most valuable cultural source of this risk by radically trans-
forming the game of street football are inviting massive mental
collapse on the national scale.

Street football—or insanity. These, then, are our alternatives.

Dr. Albert Roault, Chairman
Department of Social Psychology
Hofstra University

NOTE: The author wishes to express appreciation to the International Broadcasting Company's Educational Foundation for
providing the grant under which this research was conducted.

(Reprinted with permission from *Psychological Abstracts*, vol.
68, [2010], p. 106)

Tuesday, July 27, 2010

Shortly before three o'clock, T.K. arrives at the address on the
back of the card. It's a classic two-story stucco house. Its paint
is a fresh, light shade of green, its windows scrubbed and shining, its red-tiled roof in excellent repair. Altogether, T.K. finds
the house somewhat disconcerting. Cleanliness and intrigue
seem so incompatible. Considering the clandestine nature of
McKay's invitation, it would have been so much more apropos

had he found himself standing in front of a run-down shanty with peeling paint, cracked windows and a roof all gaping with holes.

Obviously, someone has been watching out the front window for T.K.'s arrival, for the door opens before he even has a chance to knock. "Please come in, Mr. Mann." Instantly, T.K. recognizes Senator Cy Abelman, the fervent anti-blood-sports congressman. Politicians rarely assume anything, however, least of all public recognition, so T.K. gets an introduction, anyway. "I'm Cy Abelman, U. S. Senator from Oregon. I'm glad you chose to come here today and hear us out."

T.K. steps inside. He throws back his hood, but keeps his cape on since the house's inefficient, fuel-starved old heating system hasn't yet managed to dispel the hours-old chill of a San Francisco morning. "I came out of curiosity, nothing more. I still don't believe what McKay said about Eddie. But I am interested in what you've got here that made him so almighty sure he was right."

"And you shall, and you shall. Will you step in here, please?" He indicates the dining room. In it is a large, real-wood table with several people seated around it. There's a tape projector set up on one end of the table, a screen against a far wall.

"May I introduce Mr. and Mrs. Leonard Harris, they chair the Northern California section of the Committee to End Blood Sports." He is a suave, elderly man, she a thin, well-kept woman. Both wear lush, matching hand-woven Peruvian sweaters as a shield against the cold. "The Harrises live here. And this is Sally Winehurst." A youngish, swarthy girl. With her dark coloring and coarse facial features, she could easily pass for Abelman's daughter. "My secretary. Ebbet McKay you already know. And Harry Deutsch." A nervous, bald-headed, emaciated man, dragging heavily on a cigarette. The pile in the ashtray in front of him indicates he's been at it for some time. He smokes with one hand, and pushes his specta-cles up higher on his nose at the same time with the other, a fruitless endeavor since every time he exhales his smoke, his glasses slip back down. "Harry works for IBC. He's the one who supplied us with the tape you're about to see." Abelman walks around the room pulling down the shades. "If you'll have a seat." He points toward an empty chair in back.

T.K. takes it.

Abelman turns on the tape projector. The tape clicks into place, a hiss issues forth from out of the projector's speaker. A random pattern of flashing lights appears on the screen, and the show begins.

Involuntarily, T.K. winces when he realizes what it is, a replay of Sunday's game against the Minutemen, specifically, that play in which Eddie Hougart was killed. It doesn't seem to be the standard television broadcast version, however. The voiceover isn't that of Timothy Enge. It's someone else, someone whose voice is lower, quieter, more intense than Enge's, and the voice isn't simply announcing what's going on. It seems to be talking to somebody. Giving someone directions.

"That voice you hear belongs to a man IBC euphemistically refers to as a programming adjuster," interjects Abelman. "He sits in the control room and watches the game on the program co-ordinator's console. He has a very specific purpose which I think will be made extremely obvious in a few moments."

Experiencing a strange sense of *déjà vu*, T.K. watches himself in the huddle, calling the play that will cost Eddie Hougart his life.

"This is the play we get Hougart," says the voice. "They're going to run a short screen pass to the center. Put your defense into a five-three-two, but don't blitz the inside line. On the snap, cover everybody but Hougart. Have your ends red-dog Mann. Hang back just far enough to make Hougart look wide open. Mann's a sucker for a quick, sure gainer, especially when he's under pressure and there doesn't look to be any danger to his receiver. He'll throw to Hougart, no doubt about it. When Hougart gets it, slip it to him in the throat. He's got bad eyes, so the glare from the streetlight in front of you ought to give you a few extra seconds. Have you got it? Nod twice if you've got it."

T.K. has moved to the edge of his chair. "Who's he talking to? Who the devil is he talking to?"

By way of an answer, Abelman points to the screen.

It shows Harv Matision, nodding twice.

On screen, T.K. takes the snap, and fades back to pass.

"Turn it off. I don't want to see any more of it," T.K. says. Abelman flips off the projector and turns on the overhead lights.

"Want to watch it again?"

T.K. shakes his head. "How did you get this?"

"Mr. Deutsch, here, stole it from a secret repository the network maintains. He took this one single play, duplicated it, and returned the original to its proper position."

"I did it because I can't go along with them any more," says Deutsch, his voice a putrid wisp of smoke. "They're out-and-out murdering someone in almost every game now. I went along with it when it was just a little manipulation here and there. I even sat still for an occasional killing. But I can't sit by and let it happen in every game, every week. I've got a wife and children. How would they get along if I went to prison?"

T.K. ignores Deutsch's emotional outburst. "What does Matision have?" he asks. "A receiver in his helmet?"

"In his head, Mr. Mann," answers Abelman, "in his head. He has a tiny receiver implanted just behind his left ear."

"How long has he had it there?" T.K. speaks very slowly.

"As nearly as we can tell, ever since he became a professional football player."

T.K. hangs his head and slaps his hand on his knee. "I can't believe this."

"I know," says the senator. "I didn't believe it either when Mr. Deutsch first came to me with it, but after having heard him completely out, I'm firmly convinced it is true. In fact, it extends far beyond Matision. There is one controlled player on every team in the league."

T.K. snaps upright. "Who is it on the Prospectors?"

"Unfortunately, Mr. Deutsch can't provide us with that information. A complete listing of all the co-operating players is in the hands of only two people—Pierce Spencer, the president of IBC, and his vice-president, Ida Moulay."

In assent, Deutsch shakes his head up and down, knocking cigarette ashes over himself in the process.

The senator continues. "I trust that you, being a professional, don't need to be told how relatively simple it would be to completely dominate a football game given two men, one on each side, under such guidance."

Numbly, once, T.K. lifts his head up and lets it drop. "Why are you telling me this? For all you know, I could be in with them. I could have one of those receivers stuck in my own head."

"We think not." Abelman sits on the edge of the table facing T.K., his feet crossed at the ankles, his arms folded. "According to Mr. Deutsch, they frequently refer to you at their staff meetings as being the type of player they could do without. As you may be aware, they prefer a more pugnacious variety of sportsman. No, we're certain you're not in league with them. As to why we're telling you this. Quite simple. You were there when this incident on the tape occurred." He points behind him, vaguely in the direction of the screen. "I suspect that the Minutemen's actions on this particular play were somewhat atypical. Am I right in assuming that you can vouch for such a fact?"

Again, T.K. nods emphatically once. "They had no reason whatsoever to suspect the screen. If they did, and if they were really defending against it, they would have covered everybody, Eddie included, and Matision would have dogged it along with his ends. It's a fine point, but to a pro, it's significant."

"Good. That's exactly what I was hoping you'd say. You see, we're taking our accusations to the Attorney General. We have the tape, but, speaking cynically, it wouldn't have been all that difficult for us to have dubbed in the sound track you heard. Mr. Deutsch won't be able to attest to the tape's authenticity since, in return for his co-operation, I've promised him that his name will be kept out of this, and that later on I'll intercede for him with the investigating authorities. Hence we need some definitive way to lend our tape credence. And you are that way. The tape, together with your interpretation of the events it portrays, will clinch it for us once and for all."

T.K. holds up his hand and spreads it palm out in Abelman's direction. "Wait a minute. This is all going by too quickly for me. McKay yesterday said something about my meeting Matision in the Superbowl this year. Is that part of their plan, too?"

"Yes, it is. Barring an unforeseen fatal or disabling accident to one or the other of you, it's a virtual certainty."

"And you want me to go to the Attorney General with you?"

"Yes, that's correct."

T.K. puts his hand to the back of his head, and ponders for a moment. He rises up. "O.K. I will."

Smiles of immense satisfaction break out all around the room.

"After Superbowl XXI," T.K. adds, and the smiles disappear.

"No," says the senator, taken aback. "We can't wait that long. We have to make our move now."

"I'll go after XXI. Not before."

"My God, that's more than five months away. We simply cannot wait that long."

"If you want me to go with you, you'll have to."

"But why? They killed your friend. Doesn't that mean anything to you?"

"Of course it does, but you've got your facts slightly twisted. They tipped off my play. That's all they did. Harv Matision killed Eddie. He's the one I have to settle with, and I don't want him taken off the street until I do."

"Don't you understand? Matision's under outside control. In any contest between the two of you, he will know things that you don't. He will be given information you don't have. He will be told beforehand exactly what you're going to do."

"Now that I'm aware of it, I can use it against him."

"You're being extremely unreasonable."

"No, Senator, not at all. I'm a football player. I make my living at it. I accept the risks involved. O.K. So there's somebody on every team with a receiver in his head. Fine. That's just one more risk I have to cope with."

Abelman tries another approach. "If you go with us, Matision will be punished. The courts will exact your retribution for you. It's not necessary for you to personally revenge your friend's death."

"To me it is."

The senator, who has risen and stands at the end of the table, grasps the back of a chair for support. "This is insane. I can't believe you're actually serious. Possibly I haven't gotten through to you. If you don't come with us, we'll go without you. Your support will help, but it's not essential. The overwhelming odds are that the Attorney General will accept our tape at face value, and, when he does, I can assure you, Matision won't be playing in any Superbowl, not this year or ever again. What do you say to that?"

"I know how slowly the law usually works. I'll gamble that it doesn't speed up this time."

"You'll be gambling your life, Mr. Mann. I hope you realize that."

"Senator, gambling my life is something I'm paid to do. On television. Every Sunday." T.K. gets up to leave. "See you around," he says on his way out the door, "after XXI."

Thursday, July 29, 2010

While Sarah takes a shower, T.K. puts in a long-distance call to his bet handler in Las Vegas. He pulls his vid-phone onto the bed, and sets it beside him on a pillow, arranging its pickup unit so that the bet handler gets a view of T.K.'s bare feet rather than his equally bare chest and midsection.

He punches in the number, and suffers through the mandatory pre-call advertising message. Because his call is long distance, he gets a full thirty seconds' worth. The commercial is for Tonetime, an ultra-sonic tooth cleaner. T.K. already has one. He considers it to be a worthwhile implement. He has enough pain as it is. He doesn't want to risk an aching tooth, besides.

The vid-phone hardly buzzes once before someone picks it up. A volume business is the bet handler's stock in trade. The quicker he answers, the quicker he covers a bet, the quicker he can hang up and let the chain start all over. "Bernie, T.K. Lay off a round one for me on Sunday's game with Atlanta."

"Which end?"

"You have to ask?"

"Right. You're covered. Ten thousand dollars on the Prospectors to win."

"And, Bernie, what're *my* odds?"

Bernie consults a sheet of paper at his side. "Six to four against."

"That high, huh?"

"You made it through too many already, T.K. Nobody lives forever." Bernie never minces words.

"Well, I got another round one says I live at least until Monday morning."

"You're covered. Anything else?"

"Harv Matision."

Bernie doesn't consult his sheet this time. "Two gets you three if he makes it."

"Four that he doesn't."

"Covered. That it?"

"That's it."

Bernie hangs up without saying good-by.

"Isn't that illegal?" It's Sarah. Fresh from the shower, she stands in the bathroom door, toweling dry her hair. It gives T.K. a perfect opportunity to partake of one of his newest-found pleasures, studying her naked body. He finds it as perfectly executed as a well-run sweep around end. Her full, thrusting breasts with their barely perceptible nipples. The slight faking outward of her stomach, the delicate rounding of her buttocks and thighs.

They became lovers after the twelfth game of the season, the Greys game, the one in which T.K. took such a merciless pounding. She had ministered to him all day Monday, sleeping over on his sofa to be near him should he need her in the night. When he awoke screaming, she had rushed to his side, her body completely exposed beneath the thin acetate of her cling-on pajamas. It had happened so naturally, so perfectly, so miraculously free of pain, that the next morning, had they not awakened in the same bed and gone through the same blissful motions again, he would have sworn he had dreamed it.

That afternoon, she had moved in permanently.

"Well, sort of," T.K. says in response to her query about his gambling.

She sits down beside him on the bed and begins to massage his shoulders, paying special attention to his right arm, the one Harv Matision dislocated. Even though the team physician set it back into position and completely repaired the damage to muscles and ligaments, it still gives T.K. an occasional twinge. "I don't see how something can be sort of illegal," she says. "It seems to me it either is or it isn't."

He twists around to give her better leverage. "A touch higher," he says. Her hands move up his shoulder blades to the base of his skull. She kneads in her knuckles, grinding them right and left, until his vertebrae give out with the sought-after pop. "It isn't illegal for other people," he explains. "It is for me because I'm a player."

"Won't that get you into trouble?"

"Not if nobody finds out about it, it won't."

She accepts that by slapping him playfully on the rear. "Now you do me," she says, rolling over onto her stomach.

He straddles her at the lower back and begins to massage her shoulders and spine.

"Has anybody ever approached you to throw a game?" she asks, her head turned sideways, making her question barely audible through the filtering of pillows and sheets.

"Do you want to know for your article or for yourself?"

"Does it matter?"

"If it's for your article, I'll go into expansive detail and toss in a few juicy quotes."

"I have a hunch you're setting me up, but I'll bite. It's for my article, so let me have the fully verbose option."

"Gladly." After pretending to check about for eavesdroppers, he whispers his answer through cupped hands. "No, I've never been approached to throw a game." She punches at him. He ignores her, and continues. "Bet handlers, both legal and otherwise, want the game kept on the up and up every bit as much as the football commissioner does. They know that people won't bet on something they don't trust. Oh, sure, a bet handler could sweeten his profit by fixing games, but over the long haul he'd only be hurting himself. No, that's one thing I can say about football. It might be tough, but it's honest."

Suddenly, as he realizes the ludicrous nature of what he's just said, he stiffens, simultaneously ceasing Sarah's massage.

"Tired?" she asks.

Without answering, he rolls off and lies down beside her so they can see one another without having to move. "Sarah, I had a meeting the other day with some people from EBS."

She breaks into a broad smile. "So, my body succeeds where my logic fails," she jokes, tickling his side. When he doesn't respond, when she sees how serious he is, she stops.

"They maintain there's one player on every team with a receiver buried in his head. According to them, a guy sits in the control room and broadcasts information to these players. If you believe them, there hasn't been an honest street football game played all season, maybe for even longer."

"That's incredible!" She sits up, crossing her legs beneath her. "And do you believe them?"

He nods. "They want me to go to the Attorney General with them."

She tilts her head. "Are you going to do it?"

"No." He makes a fist of one hand and smacks it idly into the other. "Harv Matision is one of the players involved." He says it as if it explains everything, though when he sees her puzzled expression, he amplifies it a bit more. "If I go with them, Matision's liable to be suspended. I don't want that to happen. You see, the EBS people told me it's all arranged. Matision and I are going to meet in XXI."

"And after XXI, you're hoping they won't have to suspend him, because you're hoping after XXI he'll be dead."

"That's blunt, but essentially true, yes."

She hops to the floor and stands there, hands on hips, addressing him as a teacher might a backward student. "Didn't it ever occur to you that it might be the other way around? It might be you who winds up dead?"

"It's occurred to me, yes."

"And you're still going through with it?"

"I'm still going through with it." He sits up, throwing his feet casually over the edge of the bed. "I want Matision. I want him more than I've ever wanted anything else in the world." His words cut through the air like a scalpel, deftly laying open his soul. "I started out wanting him for Eddie, but not any more. Now it's for me. I want him for myself. Because he made me feel old. Because he made me feel inadequate. Because he made me feel I wasn't fit any more to play football."

He grips her by the shoulders and pulls her to him, until their foreheads are almost touching. "Sarah, you have to understand why I'm doing this. It's important to me that you do." He struggles to attach a label to the unfamiliar emotion inside him. "I think I'm in love with you."

By way of response, she pulls him to her and kisses him, but neither of them really enjoys it much. It's a kiss too filled with the salty premonition of tears.

Thursday, July 29, 2010

"You're sure?" the senator asks.

"Absolutely." Sarah twists the vid-phone cord into a loop, holding an end between each thumb and forefinger. "He won't go to the Attorney General." She snaps the cord straight.

"Very well." The senator places his fist to his mouth, and

exhales into it, as if trying to trap his ideas as they spring from his head. "Let me know the very instant you feel he may be ready to waver."

A rare trace of affection creeps into Sarah's voice. "He would be a great asset to us, Senator."

"I have a strong hunch that someday soon he will be, Sarah."

She hangs up smiling, for she knows from long experience how rarely her employer is wrong.

SUPERBOWL XXI, THE GAME

Saturday, January 1, 2011, 6:00 A.M.

The promising glow of sunup breaks through the swirling snow like a match head come to ignite the gaseous cloud that is darkness. Shadows, the long shadows of morning, trail off the players like giant pointing fingers making it that much harder to elude pursuit, to escape or to hide. Fatigue seems to worsen at daybreak, to press down as if it were a tangible substance that can be carried about quite easily so long as its bearer can't see it.

The two teams begin the second quarter at equal strength, both down two men. T.K. has spent the entire first quarter, not trying to kill Matision, but rather evaluating him, gauging his strengths, balancing them off against his weaknesses. Now, at last, he's ready to put his findings to work. He assigns himself to the middle linebacker slot, the best position from which to get Matision. He watches Matision closely, keying his own actions to Matision's. Matision's a clever tactician. He calls audible after audible at the line, changing his plays to adjust for the Prospectors' beefed-up defenses. It's almost phenomenal how well he anticipates what he's going to face. At least T.K. would have thought so had he not known about the receiver in the man's skull. Now he's more inclined to attribute the majority of

Matision's precognitive maneuvers to the wonders of wireless communications rather than to a supposedly instinctive football expertise.

One thing that T.K. has noticed, whenever Matision is going to throw long, he drops back, with his right arm, his throwing arm, cocked, and his right shoulder down. As T.K. knows from long hours of viewing game tapes, Matision has a very quick release, but has a hard time holding accuracy over distance. And no amount of off-street coaching can help him with that. Apparently this style of throwing is his new way to try and boost his precision without sacrificing rapid delivery. It's also a sure tip-off that he'll be spending the slightest bit more time in possession of the ball while his receivers dash downstreet. That, by extension, makes him a good candidate for a rush. Hence, having uncovered this key indicator in Matision's behavior, T.K. waits patiently for him to do it again.

On the third play of the series, after two short, ineffectual slant outs, he finally does.

Matision takes the snap, and drops back, right arm cocked, shoulder down.

T.K. is on him like a madman, literally sailing over the backs of two blockers to get there. Even while still in the air, he has his knife out and gripped in the in-fighting position, forefinger closest to the blade for maximum reach, thumb hooked over the upper portion of the guard for stabilization.

He comes in at an awkward angle, though, catching Matision around the neck with his left hand, unable to get in a clear shot with his knife-wielding right. Matision cagily drops to one knee, and shakes him off.

T.K. does a sideways recovery roll, and grabs on again.

The two fall to the ground in a mass of flailing arms and legs.

Matision's referee blows his whistle.

But T.K. doesn't get up. Instead, he bends back Matision's head, and slips his knife in under his helmet. Matision's eyes widen, not out of fear, but wonder. Knifing after the whistle is his trick, not T.K.'s. "The whistle," he croaks, his chin strap digging into his larynx. "The whistle blew, you son of a bitch."

"Do tell," whispers T.K. straight into his ear. "And I suppose you picked it up in stereo. One channel out here on the field, another through that gadget you've got in your head. The one that helped you kill Eddie."

Now Matision's eyes do fill with terror. "I . . . I don't . . ."

"Mann," shouts Matision's referee, "you've got two seconds to disengage. One . . ."

"I'll be seeing you," whispers T.K. Guiding it with his fingertips, he flips his knife up, scoring a thin line under Matision's throat, not enough to draw blood and a penalty, just enough to aggravate, to give Matision a reminder he's vulnerable, and that there's someone who wants him. Badly. And for good reason.

T.K. hops to his feet.

On the next play, inexplicably, Matision fumbles.

The Prospectors recover, and press off on a long downstreet drive.

Monday, August 2, 2010

Corporate vice-presidents for finance, personnel, marketing, advertising and public relations each, in turn, stand and recapitulate their last week's contribution to the health and welfare of the International Broadcasting Company. Such reports, no matter how glowing, are invariably subjected to extensive dismemberment in Pierce Spencer's mangling hands. But today Spencer listens to them in unresponsive silence. He appears somehow disjoined from his staff meeting, somehow indifferent and removed, as if he has other matters, more important than last week's status of his empire, to consider. One after another, his vice-presidents report, await their traditional grueling cross-examination, then, when it's not forthcoming, sink blankly to their chairs, their expressions, every one, a mixture of surprise and relief, the condemned jerked at the last moment from in front of the firing squad and presented with a one-week reprieve.

Only when the progression of speakers reaches Ida Moulay does Spencer evince any interest whatsoever in the proceedings.

Lighting a fresh cigar, he addresses her. "You've been in contact with the SFL Owners' Association." It's not so much a question as a declarative statement of fact.

She rises, clutching a thick writing tablet, completely filled with notations. "Yes. I have my findings summarized here. If it's all right with you, I'll brief you on them verbally now, and follow up with a typed report later this afternoon." She's dealing from her most valuable strength, a profound understanding of what makes Pierce Spencer happy. She could easily have presented him with a typed report here at the meeting, but she's been around him long enough to know he detests written reports. Not so much because they're time-consuming as because he can't skin a report open on the spot, humiliate it for its nakedness, and tack its bloody hide to the wall. So Ida forgoes by choice the detached safety of the printed word in favor of the direct verbal gamble. To her, it's an even enough trade-off. She lays her self-respect on the line in return for a high six-figure income.

Spencer waggles his cigar at her, a sign that she takes to indicate his acquiescence.

"I approached the Owners' Association with your suggestion that they double the number of SFL franchises to sixty-four and play games on Fridays as well as Sundays. I explained that in such an eventuality, we would cover both days' games live, and rerun Friday highlights on Mondays, Sunday highlights on Wednesdays." She flips to her second sheet.

"I'm still not really sure we want to go through with this," Harry Deutsch interjects. Around IBC it's an open topic of debate, as well as the subject of more than one betting pool, as to just how much longer Pierce Spencer will tolerate Harry Deutsch. "I've mentioned this before, and I want to reiterate it now. I question whether there's the viewership potential to make a second night of football profitable."

Spencer saves Ida the trouble of answering. "Deutsch, if we

show enough blood, we could make a twice-weekly lecture on butterflies profitable."

Around the conference table it gets the hearty chuckle its origin commands.

Even though Spencer has effectively quashed Deutsch's objection, still, since the whole concept is Spencer's idea, Ida feels a certain imperative to justify it nonetheless. "Since most unionized workers can option for either Friday or Monday off on their four-day week, I don't think viewership will be a problem. Oh, there'll be a lot of tired people dragging in to work on Monday mornings, but that's not our concern. At any rate, it appears quite likely the owners will vote on our proposal at their winter meeting in February. Assuming they concur, which, given our liberal profit-sharing deal, would seem to be a virtual certainty, I think we can look for an expanded schedule in 2012, 2013 at the latest. Are there any questions?"

Spencer has one. "What about the arms bill lobby?"

Ida stays on her feet. "To appease the players, in public the owners will continue their support of the Abelman bill. Privately, however, they'll help us in the drive to pass Barin's increased armaments measure. Their spirit and financial support are firmly on our side."

"Good."

Ida sits down. She is the last speaker on the agenda. At this point, the staff meeting usually adjourns, but, as prior events would suggest, this is not a usual staff meeting.

Slowly, powerfully, Pierce Spencer stands, a king rising up to the height of his omnipotence, from there to address his minions. "I have one further item of business." He moves around the table, puffing on his cigar, slapping the back of each person's chair as he passes.

"I have it on reliable authority that our friend Senator Abelman was able to procure a voiced-over tape of a play from a recent game, specifically the Hougart incident in the Prospectors and Minutemen match." His hand slaps the chair three down from Harry Deutsch, then two, then one. He slaps Deutsch's chair, and there he stops. "I'm sure we can all guess what he plans to do with that tape, but that's not what concerns me. I'll deal with Abelman when the time comes. What I want to know is where he got the tape in the first place. Can anyone tell me?" He knees the back of Deutsch's chair so hard that he sends the man careening into the side of the table. "Perhaps you, Deutsch, perhaps you can tell me."

Deutsch begins to shake. He reaches out to the table and picks up his glasses, knocked off by the force of his impact. "I . . . I don't know, Mr. Spencer. I can't help you. I'm sorry."

Spencer takes Deutsch by the shoulders and pulls him forcefully back into his chair. "So am I, Deutsch, so am I."

Spencer leans across to the table, and grinds his cigar out on the cover of Deutsch's monogrammed vinyl notebook. The heat-tortured cover puckers up with a crackle and an obnoxious odor. Then Spencer wheels about and storms out of the conference room.

Wednesday, August 4, 2010

As might be expected when a controversial United States Senator lets leak the tantalizing promise that at 9 A.M. Wednesday morning he will present the Attorney General with conclusive proof that the *de facto* national sport is homicidally rigged, by eight-fifty, the Attorney General's outer office is packed with newsmen. Crammed in shoulder to shoulder, they jostle amongst themselves, vying for a position along that route from entry portal to office door, the path Senator Abelman will tread, perhaps spewing quotes in his wake. Most of the newsmen carry fist-sized press cameras. A few are outfitted for full TV transmission. All have transcription packs and directional mikes.

At Senator Abelman's request, a precious few of their number have been allowed inside the Attorney General's office itself under the stipulation their coverage be made equally available to all waiting outside.

The Attorney General, C. Clayton Wilkes, a shrewd politician and a front-runner for his party's nomination in the next presidential election, has consented to conduct his meeting with Senator Abelman in such a circuslike atmosphere primarily so as to be assured of forefront portrayal in the wide press exposure Abelman's rather sensational charges are certain to draw.

At promptly 9 A.M., shoving a curtain of "No comments at this time" in front of him, Senator Abelman pushes his way into the Attorney General's office.

Assured by his aide that the pool pressmen are all in place, the Attorney General nods to Senator Abelman. "Cy," he says, "it's your show."

Senator Abelman, no slouch himself when it comes to courting the press, faces the cameras rather than the Attorney General. "Mr. Wilkes," he intones in his most sepulchral tones, "it is my unpleasant duty to inform you that each and every street football game played in this country thus far this year has been blatantly rigged through the unscrupulous efforts of high officials of the International Broadcasting Company." His statement, while certainly coming as no surprise in light of his earlier intimations, still evokes shufflings of astonishment from the assemblage of newsmen. After skillfully letting the shifting play itself out, Abelman goes on. "There exists one player on every SFL team with a micro-receiver surgically implanted behind his ear. This player is, in each case, fed pertinent game information from the television control room, thus permitting him to accomplish greatly enhanced feats of football legerdemain." With that, he pauses for added emphasis, his head drooped, his hands lifeless at his sides. "At least one player, possibly more, has been brutally murdered as a direct result of this onerous IBC intervention."

By this time, the Attorney General, like everyone else in the room, hangs on Abelman's every word. When it becomes clear that, for the time being at least, Abelman is finished speaking, slowly, deliberately, the Attorney General interjects the obvious question. "Those are pretty serious charges, Cy. I trust you have something concrete with which to back them up."

"I do," says Abelman, pulling out his tape. "If you'll slip this into a playback machine for me."

The Attorney General presses a button atop his desk. A tape playback unit glides up from out of a recessed panel in his desk top. Concurrently, a screen slides down a far wall. He takes the tape, and drops it into the machine. He presses a button, the lights dim and the tape clicks into place.

"This tape was recorded in the IBC control room during last Sunday's Prospectors-Minutemen game," explains Abelman in an undertone. "Pay particular attention to the voice you hear on it. It's that of an IBC employee."

On the screen, T.K. Mann huddles his teammates around him. He nods his head several times, they all give what appears to be a token cry of mutual encouragement, and break for the line.

Immediately, Abelman, who has watched the tape countless times, knows that something is wrong. The programming adjuster's voice, which comes in during the huddle, is absent on this run-through. Abelman attributes it to some problem with the playback unit's sound circuitry, and calls it to the Attorney General's attention. "Clay, would you check the sound . . . ?"

A voice on the tape interrupts him. "Camera number two," it says. "Pull back, will you? They're running a short screen pass to center this play. I want you to cover Mann. Camera eight, follow the center. Camera twelve, pick up the receiver if it goes to somebody else. Camera six, give me a tight close-up of Matision." The scene cuts to a shot of Harv Matision, nodding twice.

On screen, T.K. takes the snap, and fades back to pass. The play is completed, and Eddie Hougart dies, without any further audio commentary.

The Attorney General flicks on the lights. "Cy," he says, his anger seething through his carefully groomed veneer, "if this is your idea of a joke."

"Clay," says Abelman, absolutely stunned, "that's not my tape."

"It's the tape you gave me."

"I don't understand. It's been switched, but that's impossible. That tape hasn't been out of my sight since I got it." Suddenly he stares at the Attorney General, for the first time realizing the horrible extent of the conspiracy facing him. "Unless it was switched here, in this office, after I gave it to you."

Understandably, the Attorney General erupts. "Cy, I deal in facts, not deluded ramblings." Deluded ramblings. It had a nice ring to it. It would sound suitably impressive and, at the same time, demeaning on the six o'clock news. "I'll thank you to get out of my office. I have *serious* business to conduct."

The newsmen are ecstatic. This is a story beyond their wildest dreams. A good portion of them are already dashing for the outer office to share their reports with their colleagues.

Shocked and disillusioned, Senator Abelman shambles toward the door.

"Senator," the Attorney General calls out brusquely after him. "You forgot something." He throws him the tape.

Abelman doesn't even try to field it. Instead, he lets it drop at his feet. "You keep it. A personal memento of a major skirmish in the campaign to subvert the human race." He goes out the door, and is immediately engulfed by the waiting, news-hungry throng.

When he's alone, the Attorney General picks up his vidphone, the one on the doubly secured, monitor-proofed band. He punches up a number. Moments later, Pierce Spencer's face appears on his screen.

"Success?" asks Spencer.

"Total and complete," answers the Attorney General. He presses a button under his desk, and a tape pops from out of a concealed slot. He holds it up to the screen.

"You know what to do with it," says Spencer.

"Indeed I do." The Attorney General punches out, turns and walks to the wall. He pulls down the cover on his office flash station, and drops the tape inside.

He closes the door. A red light winks on and off. When he reopens the door, there is nothing left of the tape save a small mound of dust. A press of a button, and even the mound disappears, sucked out into the atmosphere, there to become indistinguishable from the trillions of other lung-searing black particles which, together, compose the hazy pall that passes for Washington's air.

SUPERBOWL XXI, THE GAME

Saturday, January 1, 2011, 9:30 A.M.

Despite a liberal coating of warming balm, T.K.'s lips are still badly chapped from the cold. In the huddle, he makes a double fist of his hands, and blows into it at the juncture of his thumbs, but the breath coming out of his mouth seems little warmer than the chilly Boston wind swirling around him, so he crosses his arms just above the wrist and sticks his hands into his armpits to heat them, instead.

Before T.K. can make his call, Varnie Pfleg gives him an observation. "The right side tackle and end are stunting, T.K." He means they're exchanging defensive assignments. Instead of going for the man directly in front of them, they're swapping off and attacking each other's man, giving them each an angular advantage. Properly handled, it's fairly effective as an occasional change of pace. It can also become a moving disaster if the offense anticipates it and runs a play directly against it. Wordlessly, T.K. acknowledges Pfleg's report. T.K. usually has great success working off stunting linemen. Normally, he would call something against it immediately. This time, though, he has other considerations. Since he still has absolutely no idea which one of his own teammates is an IBC dupe, he has to weigh each and every suggestion not only for individual merit but for possibly hidden implications as well.

He racked both his brain and the statistics book for weeks after first finding out there was a controlled player on his team, but all to no avail. D'Armato had the highest kill ratio on the team, but then, that wasn't particularly unusual for a hidden safety. Orval Frazier was far and away the most aggressive player, but he worked mainly with his bare hands. He didn't use his knife much, nor did he kill many of his opponents, and, as T.K. understood it, that would make him less than an ideal choice by IBC standards. The rest of them, Pfleg, Minick, Brye, Clausen, Dedemus, DeGeller, Michalski, Healy and Howe all had their moments of brilliance, but they had their share of off days, too. Which left T.K. as much in the dark as ever.

T.K. puts his hands on his knees and bends over. "Check with me at the line." They break and line up.

T.K. has been calling almost every play at the line ever since that disastrous run in the first quarter that resulted in his almost losing Frazier. While T.K. can't prevent Matision's getting relayed knowledge concerning players' actions and locations after the ball has been snapped, he can, by calling all his plays only seconds before they're executed, at least deny Matision advanced access to that important bit of information.

T.K. studies the defense. Deprived of electronic intelligence, Matision has turned to the traditional defensive technique of keying, concentrating intently on T.K.'s actions, trying to read from their sum total what T.K. is about to do so he can react accordingly. To throw off Matision's timing, T.K. counters with a head, hip or shoulder fake just prior to receiving the ball.

As Pfleg said, the right side tackle and end are almost imperceptibly leaning in each other's direction, usually a certain indication of a stunt. T.K. weighs it, but decides to ignore it. To the Prospectors, it's common knowledge how much he enjoys working against such a tactic, and it could be a setup. Even if Pfleg isn't wired up, it's a safe bet the control room picked up his comment on a directional mike and by now it's probably been relayed to Matision. Best to stay away from it. Instead, he calls for a long pass to Michalski. "Red six, one, three, five." Healy centers him the ball.

Instinctively, T.K. grabs it, turning it so his fourth and little fingers cover the lacing, his middle finger lies almost exactly midway down the taper, his forefinger almost on the end, and his thumb encircles it, facing off at an angle just below its point of widest circumference. He drops back into his protective pocket of blockers, sets and sees Michalski in the clear. He's already got the football next to his ear. He releases it from there. It sails, spiraling and true, right into Michalski's waiting arms. Michalski feints around a potential tackler, leapfrogs across a low, decorative railing in front of an antiquated apartment house, and cuts inside the building.

Leaving Michalski to his own devices, T.K. sprints for the goalyard.

There he waits, in vain as it turns out.

His referee taps him on the shoulder. "South Russell and Myrtle, Mann. Play's all done."

T.K. trods on over. When he arrives, he finds Rauscher hunched above Michalski, who is bleeding from his nose and his ears. Rauscher gives T.K. a sign. Thumb down. Michalski is out for the rest of the game.

"Who got him?" T.K. asks in the huddle.

"Who else?" answers Buddy Healy. "The fabulous one-man football team."

T.K. glances back at the defense to see Harv Matision wiping his knife blade clean on his jersey.

At least Michalski didn't go out in vain. He made eighty-two yards on the play, giving the Prospectors a badly needed first down.

"Check with me at the line," T.K. says.

They break and go into formation.

Monday, September 6, 2010

The Prospectors' locker room is in a state of near pandemonium. Players in various stages of undress pound each other on the back and shoulders with inflatable plastic casts filled with water, throw squishy oranges and wads of blood-splattered tape at each other, or douse each other liberally with beer.

Needless to say, the reason for all this riotous joviality is a victory, a victory over Chicago. This victory, coupled with a

Seattle defeat, leaves the Prospectors in undisputed first place in their division, and heirs to a one week's bask in the glory of pre-eminence.

T.K., as has been his pattern lately, doesn't join his comrades in their after-game buffoonery. Instead, he sits sullenly in front of his locker, stripping off first his uniform, then his pads, his tape and finally his iron horse. He grabs a towel from the trainer, and heads for the showers, roughly shoving aside two network cameramen who are blocking his way.

As he reaches the shower, he hears a familiar voice calling to him. Senator Cy Abelman, looking rumpled and damp, there being no way to pick through this jostling crowd of athletes without acquiring a thin layer of perspiration in the process, emerges from out of the jubilant ruckus. T.K. isn't surprised to see a United States Senator here. A good public relations man can open all manner of doors, including the one on a football team's locker room; hence, after a game, particularly after a winning game, dignitaries and celebrities, anxious to be seen on television in the company of a victor, usually cram inside. However, since Senator Abelman has gone frequently on record as being above such cheap shot publicity, T.K. deduces it's something other than a wish for media exposure that drew him here today.

The senator removes a large red bandanna from his shoulder bag and does as good a job as he can of mopping the droplets of sweat from his cape. "I've been trying to buzz you up at home, but I can never seem to get through."

T.K. hangs his towel on a hook outside the shower entrance. "My answering service screens for me during the season. I get a lot of calls from people trying to sell me one thing or another."

"I'm sure. But still, I'm hardly a . . ." Abelman gets T.K.'s meaning. His messages were received, all right, just never answered. "Never mind. You heard what happened to me at the Attorney General's office, I suppose."

T.K. reaches in and turns on a shower. "I couldn't help it. It was on every newscast and in all the papers." He gives the senator a firm, appraising glance. "You know, you look a lot better in real life than you do in the media."

"I was conned. The Attorney General is in on the whole thing. I suspect he's trading his co-operation for media support in the forthcoming election."

"So you're the man with the quick solution. Go somewhere else. Try the football commissioner. Or the President. I hear he's quite a football fan. He'd probably love to sit through your act." T.K. steps inside the shower, letting icy cold water cascade down his back and across his buttocks.

"The point is, I can't go someplace else. My original tape disappeared—I suspect the Attorney General has destroyed it by now. I can't get another one since, as I understand it, shortly after this one was stolen from them, the network ceased the production of all such incriminating records and also, as a precautionary measure, destroyed all the ones remaining in their files."

"Well, put the pressure on your squealer, then. The Deutsch guy."

The senator takes a long time to respond. "Deutsch is dead."

T.K.'s eyes are filled with soap, so he can't see Abelman's face, but the senator's ominous tone indicates he's not altogether convinced everything was strictly aboveboard with the way Deutsch expired.

Abelman goes on. "Deutsch died last week. Ostensibly, he suffered a heart attack at his desk the day after I saw the Attorney General, and lapsed into a coma from which he never recovered. He was given an autopsy—by the IBC president's personal physician, strangely enough—and that was it. Massive heart arrest, says the report, but I'm not convinced. His death was too neatly timed to have been a coincidence." Risking a sound drenching, the senator sticks his head inside the shower to insure T.K. can hear him above the sound of the running water. "It might interest you to know that IBC is providing nothing, not so much as a nickel, to his wife and children."

"Indecent bastards, aren't they?" T.K. scrubs off his head,

turns off the water and sticks his hand outside. "Hand me my towel, would you?"

Abelman does.

T.K. dries off his head, neck and shoulders. He's halfway down his chest before he speaks. "The answer is no."

"The answer to what?"

"Let's not be coy, Senator. We both know why you're here. The answer is no, I won't go with you to see whomever you've decided to go to see next. Not until after the Superbowl." T.K. sits down on a bench, takes a hot medicated towel from out of a nearby sterilizer, and wraps it around his face, making particularly sure it covers the bleeder wounds on his neck. No sooner does he have it in place, though, than Abelman, in a rare fit of anger, rips it off.

"That's insane. That's criminally insane. These network people aren't simply rigging games. They're killing people. People other than football players. Deutsch. I'm positive they killed Deutsch. You can't ignore that."

Calmly, T.K. rewraps his face, leaving his mouth open. "I can, and I will."

Senator Abelman leans in closer so his voice will penetrate through the layers of cloth. "Even though it means innocent people will die?"

"They would have died anyway, whether I knew about this or not."

"But now you can prevent it."

"And after the Superbowl, I will."

Justice for one before justice for all. It's inequitable, sure, but equity isn't one of the rules in T.K.'s game of life. Retribution. Retribution is a rule, maybe the cardinal rule, that and vengeance, swift and bitter. IBC is behind it all, but IBC is a big, impersonal corporation. Harv Matision, on the other hand, is something T.K. can see, smell, hate and, yes, best of all, destroy. But how does one go about explaining that, explaining the whole concept of manhood to a man with negotiations for balls. T.K. strips the cloth from his face. "That's my final word, Senator. After the Superbowl. Not one minute before."

Senator Abelman, completely drained of arguments, lowers his head and walks away.

A cameraman pans after him, following him out of the locker room door. This shot, plus one before of him talking to T.K., plus an audio pickup of their entire conversation is all fed into the control room, still active for the after-game color.

The programming adjuster watches it on the master console, listens to it through his multi-channeled earphones, and immediately picks up a vid-phone, a bright green one, the direct line to Pierce Spencer.

"Mr. Spencer," he says when his employer answers, "there's something I think you should know."

> Visual: The IBC logo, a football overlaying stylized
>   representations of a knife and a rifle.
> Announcer: Catch all the action, all the time, right here on
>   IBC, your street football network.

(The preceding message is broadcast on the half hour every single day of the year.)

Monday, September 6, 2010

Methodically, with all the persistence of a metronome cast in the shape of a fist, Pierce Spencer hammers his desk with his hand.

Bam. "Damn that son of a bitch." Bam. "That miserable bastard." Bam. "First Abelman, now Mann." Bam. "I'm surprised he didn't print up a faxsheet and pass it out on street corners.

All the while he rants, Ida Moulay sits pristinely off in one corner of his office, acting as a sounding board for his rage. She doesn't interject any opinions of her own, nor, in this situation, is she expected to. Working out seemingly insurmountable problems is a technique Pierce Spencer has raised to the level of high art, and, like most artists, he enjoys displaying his talent to a receptive public. Hence Ida Moulay. A smile at the right moment, a nod of assent, an admiring wrinkle of the brow, a subtle underscore to the artistic ego.

"I took care of Deutsch." The bastardly son of a bitch referred to earlier. "I turned Abelman into a laughingstock. Now I've got to deal with Mann."

At this point in his cognitive processes, if Pierce Spencer is even aware that he's not alone in this room, he gives scant indication. He talks loudly off into space, as a god might address the billowing clouds around him out of which he will fashion a whole new world. "Thus far, I've promoted this thing between Mann and Matision as a battle between youth and experience." His eyes partially close, his mouth draws tightly together. "Maybe it's time to start promoting it as a contest between competence and incompetence, instead. I understand T.K. Mann is quite proud of his abilities as a football player. Maybe it's time he received a sobering dose of humility. Yes, maybe it's time he learned how easily a reputation can flutter and die. Yes, I think that shall be my strategy, that coupled, perhaps, with a counseling session. Yes, definitely, couple that with a counseling session. Ida"—she jerks to attention—"get me our confidential file on Mr. T.K. Mann."

Saturday, September 11, 2010, 2:00 A.M.

". . . and so this doctor says to her, now that we got your nose taken care of, we'll start to work on your ears."

It's met by a few groans and a weak chuckle. The audience tonight in the Crown Room of the Royal Court Hotel, a modern New York City landmark built astride Grand Central Station, is far more interested in liquor and drugs than in comic entertainment, even when the comedian is Percy Bysshe, renowned TV personality.

"Wheeze if you're still alive out there," he says.

As everything before, it draws nothing, so, in desperation, he decides to abandon his basic slapstick patter for something new, a topical bit his writers put together only four days ago at the insistence of somebody from his network's top management. He's never tried it in front of an audience before, but it can't do any worse than anything else he's done tonight, so he gives it a whirl.

"Hey, and what about that Senator Abelman?" To his great surprise, the mention of Abelman's name draws his first real reaction of the night, a chorus of boos from the crowd. Not quite sure exactly what it is they're booing, he becomes quite tentative in his follow-up, ready to back off the instant the crowd grows ugly. "I understand he's uncovered a new plot in the SFL. According to the good senator, the players all have bugs on their balls."

The crowd loves it. They break up.

"I understand if the Abelman bill passes, the players won't be able to use weapons any more. Hell, you take away their knives, clubs and guns, and what does that leave them? I can see it now. Thirteen men out there on the street pissing on each other."

That one really gets them. Whistles, cheers and bellowing laughter.

"Hey, that T.K. Mann has been around a long time, hasn't he?" A sparse round of applause. "He's been on the operating table so many times, I hear his teammates call him Zipperhead."

Several people in the audience start laughing so steadily and so hard, Bysshe's next few lines are almost buried.

"They say T.K. Mann is pressuring the Prospectors to replace their mediman for him. With a geriatrician."

At this, there's not an unlaughing patron in the house.

"You talk about the problems of an old football player, T.K. Mann has had his skin tightened up so many times that he wears his pecker for a necktie."

He lets the laughter build, then hits them with a zinger to reinforce it. "And if you think that's bad, you should see where his nose wound up." He pats himself on the fanny.

He keeps punching away at it: Senator Abelman, the folly of altering football, and a decrepit, doddering old quarterback name of T.K. Mann.

At the end of his act, he leaves with a standing ovation.

SUPERBOWL XXI, THE GAME

Saturday, January 1, 2011, 11:30 A.M.

The second quarter runs out without the Prospectors scoring. What's more, Varnie Pfleg and Lester Brye are both put permanently out of the game, Pfleg with a severed knee ligament, Brye with a spinal fracture. This leaves only Orval Frazier, still, in spite of massive injections of procaine and biembutal, undergoing intense pain from his broken arm, Hellinger Clausen, Ken Dedemus, Ros DeGeller, Buddy Healy, Gus D'Armato, T.K., and, of course, Zack Rauscher. Eight men left out of thirteen. T.K. has played with only eight active players before, but always at points far later in the game. (In actual fact, starting the third quarter with eight men earns the Prospectors a line in the SFL record book.)

The only bright side to the Prospectors' situation is that the Minutemen aren't much better off. Thanks to some very fine defensive work by Frazier and D'Armato, four Minutemen are permanently out of the game, putting the Prospectors at only a one-man disadvantage. All in all, the situation isn't as bad as it could be.

Although you'd never know it by listening to Coach Carrerra.

"God damn it," he rants in the locker room, "you are giving this game away. Handing it to those bastards on a wooden platter." Hands waving in the air, he paces the locker room's length. "What is the matter with you today? Matision is reading our every move. He's six steps ahead of us on almost every play. Frazier, D'Armato, I want Matision stopped, and I want him stopped hard." He halts his pacing in front of T.K. "T.K., do you have your play book handy?"

Wearily, T.K. pulls it from his locker and holds it up.

"O.K. You've still got a few minutes. Refamiliarize yourself with the eight-man patterns. Run five men on the line, split your ends, and go to a spread T, two back, one over. This next quarter, I want you to run more outside buttonhooks. Put your receivers into escape positions. Hit them closer to the side-walks. Lead them back into the side streets. Stay cool, and, above all, don't give up. It's only fourteen points. We've got half a game left. We can win this son of a bitch yet."

Comes a knock on the locker room door. "Coming up on twelve-thirty. Let's play ball."

T.K. rallies his remaining seven players around him, and, in a tight knot, they hit the street running.

Harv Matision takes the kickoff and ducks south down Joy Street.

T.K. hand-signals his teammates to slice across to Walnut to cut off the long gainer, while he heads after Matision to try for the intercept.

He manages to keep Matision in sight, and even to shorten the distance between them somewhat, when, suddenly, he turns a corner, and Matision is gone. There are no alleys on either side of the street, so he's gone into a building. But which one?

Automatically, T.K. checks the snowbanks on either side of the street looking for fresh footprints, but the snow is hard-packed, almost ice, and tells him nothing.

This is the type of situation that players dread. Should he wait, hoping to pick up a trace of movement, or, assuming Matision will stick to ground floors in a bid to gain yardage, set off on a random building-to-building search?

Factoring in Matision's hidden advantage, his built-in connection to the control room, T.K. decides to sit tight, banking on his suspicion that IBC, eager for a confrontation between him and Matision, will eventually bring the two of them together. He hunkers down in a doorway, tucks his hands up under his armpits and out of the cold, and waits.

He doesn't have to wait long.

A movement catches his eye, an almost imperceptible flicker of motion inside the entrance to the five-story Institute of Contemporary Art halfway down the block. T.K. makes directly for the Institute's door. It's locked, but made of glass, so he smashes it in with his fist, opens it and steps inside. The burglar alarm goes off with a wail, but T.K. doesn't care. He knows full well he'll never be able to surprise Harv Matision. Not during this game.

In the foyer, T.K. pauses, pressed against the wall. He sees nothing. He moves on down a nearby corridor, and stops again. Still nothing. He's almost ready to move on further when he hears a sound, a slushing counterpoint to the burglar alarm's wail, a slap on marble. Then he hears it again. And yet again. Slap, slap, slap, slap, slap. The wet piston sound of a man running.

He charges down the corridor, rounds a corner, and almost smashes into Harv Matision.

Matision reacts quickly, kicking out with his foot, catching T.K. in the ribs. T.K. stumbles backwards, swiftly regains his balance and pulls out his long knife. Matision sets off up a nearby flight of stairs in search of a better defensive location. T.K. follows hot on his heels.

Halfway up the stairs, Matision rips a painting from the wall, and scales it down at T.K. In a brilliant swirl of blue, gray and green, it zips by his head.

T.K.'s referee promptly throws down a yellow and black checkered flag. Penalty. Offensive use of a weapon. The stunt will cost the Minutemen fifteen yards at the play's conclusion.

T.K. dodges the painting, barely slowing down in his dash up the stairs. He reaches the top, spots Matision, and chases after him.

Matision turns a corner. T.K. hears a door slam, rounds the same corner, and comes up to the end of the corridor. There's a single, thick, windowless door in front of him. He tries it. It won't open. Matision's either locked or barricaded it from the inside.

But why? A quick scan tells T.K. there's no other door leading out of that room. Matision has to move the ball. If he spends
more than ten minutes in there, the play will be called dead.
Ahead by only fourteen points, it's hardly likely he'd go for a
ten-minute stall. That means that, appearances to the contrary,
he does have a way out. T.K. visualizes the building's outside.
It's a standard chromagian affair. No outside fire escapes. No
covered porticoes. Just granite slabs heaped atop one another
separated only by blank rows of windows. Of course! Windows.
And underneath each window, a narrow granite ledge.

T.K. enters the first open door he comes to, runs to the window, smashes it open, and sticks his head outside. Sure enough,
there, not twelve feet away from him, is Harv Matision, carefully inching his way along, making for the corner of the building, where a series of granite indentations ladder their way
straight from the ledge to the ground.

Realizing he can never catch Matision by going down the
stairs and out the door, T.K. slips through the window and hops
onto the ledge himself.

Matision's back is pressed to the wall. The football, stuffed
into his gut pocket, sticks straight out ahead of him, giving him
a decidedly pregnant appearance. Seeing T.K. coming after
him, he tries to move faster, but the ledge is coated with ice
and, in spite of the suction cups on his shoes, he can't increase
his speed much above a slow sideways shuffle.

T.K. has his stomach pressed to the wall, his arms spread-
eagled, his heels hooked over the ledge's edge. Unencumbered
by the football, he moves faster than Matision, and, as a result,
catches him before he can reach the corner.

T.K. passes his long knife from his right hand to his left, the
hand closest to Matision. He makes a tentative jab in Matision's
direction. Matision parries with his own left hand, at the same
time kicking out with his left foot. T.K. grabs for it, misses, and
in the process, loses his balance. He plants himself, but his right
foot hits a patch of ice. It careens out from under him, skidding
backwards over the ledge. He drops straight down, barely man-
aging to catch the ledge in time to prevent a fall. He hangs on

by his fingertips, his toes searching in vain for the slightest hold.

Matision, seeing his plight, reverses direction and inches his way back to him. T.K. makes one last, desperate effort to pull himself up before Matision can reach him, but fails. Matision sidles over him, glares down, smiles and, putting all his might behind it, stomps on T.K.'s fingers.

T.K. sails backwards through the air, twisting around to improve his position for the fall. He hits the ice-covered ground with a bone-crunching snap.

The next thing he sees is Zack Rauscher hunched over him. T.K.'s left arm hurts worse than anything he's ever known before. His sleeve has been ripped off, his left arm guard removed. He's completely covered, head to toe, with a white, quilted, red-crossed blanket. Zack is preparing to give him an injection.

"How bad is it?" T.K. asks.

"Your arm is broken at the shoulder, elbow and wrist." Zack plunges the needle home. "I'm sorry, T.K., but I'm afraid you're out of the game."

Monday, October 4, 2010

The poetry of intimidation is a rhymed couplet, one line of degradation, meted out with careful rhythmic precision over several weeks, and one of blunt confrontation, as exemplified by the infamous Pierce Spencer counseling session.

T.K. has had an adequate sampling of degradation. For two weeks he's been artfully and mercilessly assailed on stages, radios and television sets across the country. Hence it's time for his counseling session to begin. Because of the nature of the leverage to be employed, T.K.'s session is to be conducted by the most persuasive counselor at Pierce Spencer's disposal.

It is slightly after noon. Sarah has gone shopping. T.K. has just poured himself his first drink of the day when his entry chime sounds. He flips on the scanner. It fills with the impressive sight of Senator Lako Barin waiting with ponderous dignity outside the door.

"What the hell, now?" T.K. mutters, electronically disengaging the lock.

Senator Barin enters. His eyes flick rapidly about the room, the hunter sizing up his quarry's lair. A sense of invasion, of impending attack hangs about the senator like the smell of gunpowder. Creases mark his face with the etched precision of battle lines scored on a soldier's map. He pushes forth his hand. "T.K. Mann. Good to meet you. I'm Senator Lako Barin."

T.K. grasps the hand in his own, pumps it up and down once, and unceremoniously releases it, as if he finds its touch somewhat revolting. "What can I do for you?" he asks, although, deep down, he can guess.

Seeing the glass in T.K.'s hand, Barin points to it. "I don't suppose you have another of those?" Senator Barin has always found alcohol helps to lubricate the wheels of diplomacy.

"Sure," says T.K. "Scotch and water all right?"

"Fine. By the way, that was some game you played yesterday. The way you pulled it out in the final hour." Barin slaps a fist into an open hand. "My God, but you can play football."

T.K. hands him his drink. "Thanks, but I have a hunch you didn't come over here to talk football."

Barin takes a sip. He is between T.K. and the glassed-in patio. The sun shining through backlights him with a flaming, almost supernatural radiance. Every time T.K. moves to block it out, the senator also moves to maintain it. Finally, T.K., mildly annoyed by the tactic, presses a button, opaquing the glass.

"Quite to the contrary," says Barin. "A discussion of football is precisely the reason I'm here. I came at the request of a mutual friend."

"A mutual friend?"

"Yes, a, shall I say, secret admirer of yours. A man with a great deal of respect for your talents and a great desire to see you enjoy life to the fullest."

T.K. mentally shades in this impressionistic sketch and, to his horror, winds up with a full-blown study in surrealism. "You're here as an emissary from IBC, aren't you?"

"You could say that, yes."

"They know that I'm on to what they're doing, then." That much is obvious. What they plan to do about it isn't quite as apparent. He can't help but remember Deutsch, although a United States Senator would seem an odd choice of assassin.

"That you're conscious of their little ploy? Of the way they add spice to the game? Yes, they're aware of your knowledge in that area. They're also cognizant of the fact that you plan to reveal your knowledge publicly immediately after the Superbowl. That is why I'm here. To offer you a powerful incentive for not doing so."

T.K. says nothing. Correctly, Barin takes his silence to be a tacit request for fuller disclosure.

"Your career is almost at an end, Mr. Mann. I don't believe you to be imprudent enough to deny that. My sources inform me you do enjoy playing the game of football very much, however, so this is my proposition. Let IBC give your career new life. Let IBC regain for you all the glories of your best years, and all at little or no risk to your own life."

T.K. sinks into his sofa, plants his legs in a wide V in front of him on the coffee table. He hangs one arm carelessly over the sofa's back, not so much for comfort as to conceal the involuntary way his hand has compressed itself into a tightly rolled fist. "You're offering to implant one of those gadgets in me."

Senator Barin drops to a chair across from him and leans forward, sincere, persuasive, the consummate salesman. "It's a short, painless operation, done in a top-rate hospital by qualified surgeons, and, of course, performed entirely at IBC expense. In addition, you'll be given a very handsome initial payment plus a lucrative monetary compensation linked to your on-street performance."

At this point T.K. has to set his drink down and throw his other hand over the sofa, too. "Senator, I'm not a puppet. I live by my wits, not by the manipulation of somebody sitting off somewhere punching my buttons. My answer to your offer is no."

It doesn't seem to come as much of a surprise to Barin. "As I assumed it would be, Mr. Mann, as I assumed it would be." With a great deal of flair, he drains his glass and sets it out on the table in front of him, as if to signify the end to his sociability. "Now I'm afraid we must go into our somewhat less pleasant alternatives. As you are undoubtedly aware, your popularity has decreased markedly in the past few weeks."

T.K. has noticed it in many obvious ways. In the almost complete petering out of his fan mail, in the decrease of requests for his autograph and his photo, even, somewhat, in the attitude of his fellow players.

"I can assure you that if you persist in your ill-advised course of action, your popularity will continue to decrease, except from here on it will do so logarithmically. To use a somewhat colorful metaphor, you will be disemboweled by the press, your bones will be bleached white from the glare of bad exposure and left to rot in the media desert. On the other hand, agree to maintain your silence, and you have my word your reputation will be restored to its formerly high-held level."

T.K.'s answer isn't long in coming, or long once it arrives. "No deal."

"You're a very stubborn individual, Mr. Mann. You force me to pursue a line of persuasion I find most repugnant." He clicks his tongue several times—it's his way of showing distaste—but he never drops his smile. "We have certain files on you, Mr. Mann. Among them we have your gambling records. Among them we have sworn testimony that you own and illegally operate an automobile. We will not hesitate to make those files public should you continue to aggravate us. I needn't remind you that you could go to jail for those offenses. Tell me, is your sense of duty more important to you than your freedom?"

"Quite frankly, yes." T.K. begins to rise, really having to try, by now, to control his temper. "If you're all through . . ."

"Hardly, Mr. Mann." Senator Barin reaches across to touch his arm, to guide him back down. "In fact, I've only begun." He reaches into his breast pocket and pulls out a thick document. "I have here a deed." He opens it and points it in T.K.'s direction, holding it firmly, top and bottom. "It's the deed to your parents' farm, the farm you now lease from the government. For a pledge of your silence, I will insure that this deed is endorsed over to you. Thereafter, you will own this property totally for all time to come."

Frankly a bit shaken by this approach, T.K. reaches for the paper, opens it, reads it. It is, indeed, the title to his parents' farm. He hands it back. Three months earlier, it would have been quite tempting, but he has higher priorities now. "Get out of here."

"I'm sorry you feel that way. You force me to put forth my final and most abhorrent argument. Even as we sit here, a team of government workers is busy laying out a ring of high explosives around this farm." He waves the paper in the air. "Ostensibly, they are blasting out an irrigation canal. But, through an unfortunate engineering error, when the explosives go off, they will blow the house, the grounds and everything on them to powder."

T.K.'s mouth hangs open.

"You can prevent this, Mr. Mann, by simply pledging me your silence." Barin, certain of victory, leans back.

Wordlessly, T.K. stands, turning his back to Barin. He lowers his head and cups it with his hands. Oddly enough, before Barin's visit, T.K. was halfway inclined to drop the whole IBC mess, anyway. Not Matision. No, he would get Matision, but, what the hell, let IBC diddle around if they wanted to. To his knowledge, they'd never directly crossed him. Not until now, at any rate, no, not until now.

Unable to contain his pent-up fury any longer, T.K. whirls, literally picks Barin up by the collar, carries him to the door and pitches him out into the hall. "As you might have guessed, Senator," he snaps at the rumpled heap of injured dignity on the floor, "the answer is no."

Barin hoists himself up, favoring his left hip, bruised in his fall. "You've got trouble, Mr. Mann. I hope you realize it. You've got big trouble."

T.K. closes the door, cutting him off from view.

When Sarah returns from her shopping trip, she finds T.K. passed out on the sofa, three empty liquor bottles lined up neatly on the table beside him.

SUPERBOWL XXI, THE GAME

Saturday, January 1, 2011, 6:15 P.M.

His world is a protracted, swirling cyclone, whisking away great chunks of complacency's breathable air, replacing it with the foggy, choking dust of long-buried remembrances.

There are his parents, two shocks of white hair, two quiet, reassuring smiles, two gentle touches, as like each other as the first breezes of two succeeding springtimes, so delicate to the appearance, yet nurturing the strength of all nature within. And there is his car. Slamming into a corner, its engine whining out the siren call of forbidden vitality. Football is wedged in there, too. It drips his ego out through the spigot of his crumbled morality. He maims and enjoys it; he kills and is proud.

Enter Harv Matision. A great shining plug-ended wire protrudes from his ankle up to a huge golden socket imbedded in the sky. Charged with the outpouring of celestial fury, Matision crackles and bristles. Nothing can touch him lest it die from the might of his aura. Matision embraces the two elderly blocks of goodness that are parents, and they shrivel away. He rubs up against the car in all its metallic fury and, as quickly as ice cream in hell, it melts to a river of slop. Last, but not least, he lays hands upon Football, and, like all else before it, that vanishes too.

Fully warmed to his ultimate task, he approaches T.K., his right index finger extended, a gesture of choosing, a volition of death.

T.K. backs away, further and further, until finally he can back up no more. He is trapped by the boundaries of his own misconceptions. Unless he can scale them, he dies. He starts to climb. A quarter of the way, a half, three quarters he passes and finally grasps to the top, but his fingers betray him. They slip, slip and give way. He tumbles headlong to the ground, his ears filled to bursting with the sound of his life rushing past him, that and Harv Matision's hideous laughter.

Then he hears something else, a voice, a far-off voice, calling to him. "T.K., wake up," says the voice, "come on, snap out of it."

Someone slaps his cheeks. Right. Left. Right again. Since there is no pain associated with it, he opens his eyes more out of curiosity than a sense of abuse.

The slapping stops. T.K. finds himself looking upward at the polished gloss that is the locker room's ceiling.

"Tell me what day it is, T.K.," demands a man, Coach Carrera, standing above him.

Strange, T.K. thinks, how so deceptively simple a request can pose such a major problem. What day is it? There are only seven. It has to be one of them. He tries to narrow his selection down somewhat. He scans his memory, backing up, day by day, until he arrives at an action he can, with a reasonable degree of certainty, link to a specific point in time. That day he scouted out the street. Wednesday. For the Superbowl. The Superbowl. Who won the Superbowl, anyway, he wonders? Then, like a torrent of slime, it engulfs him. "Saturday," he answers. "It's Saturday, January first."

"Good." The coach leans out of his field of vision to address someone else. "I don't think he's got a concussion, Zack. How about you?"

Zack, good old Zack, bends into T.K.'s constricted universe and prods at his temples. "I agree. Apparently no brain damage. He should get to the hospital as soon as possible, though. In addition to the break, the fall splintered his arm guard. He has fragments of it embedded like shrapnel. Here, and here."

T.K.'s arm moves, although he can't feel anyone touching it.

"Tell me about the game," he whispers, but Zack and Coach Carrerra are once more somewhere off to one side and can't hear him. He attempts to turn his head, but it refuses to respond. Only then does he realize he's strapped, head, chest and legs, to the training table. He has wires running off his cheekbones and, judging by the feel, off his crown and the back of his skull as well. Out of the corner of his eye, he can make out a bank of analytical instruments, their gauges, needles and lights flashing and flickering with his every movement. Reflected in the polished chrome reflectors on the ceiling he can see Zack and Coach Carrerra examining the red squiggles on a strip chart recording gushing forth from a squatty machine.

"You're right, Zack," says the coach, tapping a cluster of peaks. "I'll get him in a jit and over to Harv Med right away."

"The game," interjects T.K. with as much insistence as he can muster. "For Christ's sakes, tell me about the game." Unfortunately, not all the words make it past his lips.

"What, the game?" says Zack inattentively. He is back to monitoring his instruments and not inclined to interrupt his work to deal with what he interprets to be an injured man's incoherent ramblings.

"Yeah, the game. What else?" responds T.K. He slurs his words badly, and they're rather difficult to make out. To gain Zack's attention, he struggles against his bonds. The needles on Zack's instruments dance wildly. Some go off scale.

"Hey, T.K. Calm down."

"Only if you tell me about the game." It comes out with thespian clarity.

Correctly figuring it to be the simplest way to keep him quiet, Zack fills him in. "We're almost ready to start the fourth quarter. They scored once more, but missed the extra, so it's twenty to nothing. They tagged us hard after you got caught. Clausen, Dedemus, Healy and DeGeller are all permanently out. We've only got three actives left."

"Four. You've still got me." He says it resolutely, as if there is no doubt.

"I'm afraid not, T.K." The jitney, siren wailing, pulls up outside. Zack unstraps him preparatory to his journey to the hospital. "Your arm is shot. I'll level with you. As bad as it is, we'll be lucky to save it. You go back out there, and I don't give it a chance."

"Zack." His chest free, T.K. sits up. The room spins around, but he fights off the nausea and remains upright, resisting Zack's frantic efforts to lay him back down. "Zack, can you strap this thing to my side? Keep it out of my way?"

"T.K., I don't think you ought to be sitting up."

"That's not what I asked you." T.K.'s voice has a stern edge to it, the no-nonsense tone of a leader, a man accustomed to having his bidding accomplished, immediately and without question. "Can you patch me up well enough to go back in there? Yes or no?"

Zack faces a curious dilemma. He may be a doctor, but he's also a football player, and, after a brief internal struggle, he subjugates his medical ethics to his athletic desire. "Well, yes, but I don't recommend . . ."

"Do it, then." T.K. twists around so his injured left side faces Rauscher directly.

"T.K., I won't be responsible for . . ."

"Do it!"

From out of his supply cabinet, Zack resignedly fetches two twenty-inch-long steel troughs. Gingerly, he slips T.K.'s drug-deadened arm into first one and then the other, so the arm is completely encased in metal. He snaps the two troughs together. He pumps a quantity of crushed foam through a series of plugs positioned in the cast at two-inch intervals. Then, by mouth, he inflates two plastic sacks running the cast's inside length. The sacks and foam will cushion a fair percentage of the impact T.K.'s arm will undergo, but certainly not all. The cast is meant to afford mediocre protection, nothing more. T.K.'s injuries are bound to be aggravated. Even T.K. has no illusions about that. Finished inflating the sacks, Zack sets about the laborious task of taping the entire contraction immobile to T.K.'s side.

Coach Carrerra returns. "Hey, what's going on here? T.K., you're in no condition to . . ."

"I'm going back in," T.K. states flatly. "How are the Minutemen doing for numbers?"

Automatically, before he can absorb the full implications of T.K.'s statement, the coach answers. "Orval and Gus have been going wild. The Minutemen only have three actives left. Same as us."

"Matision?"

"Yes, him, Bumbo Johnson, and their mediman."

"They still got their bullet?"

"No. They used it to get Clausen."

"We still got ours?"

Coach Carrerra nods. Filled with reservations as to the wisdom of T.K.'s decision, he makes one last attempt to dissuade him. "Don't go back in there. I'm your coach. I want to win this one as much as you do, but there comes a time when the only logical thing to do is to hang up your horse. This game is as good as lost. Let's think about next year, instead. Save yourself for the future. There's no way you can do us any good out there, T.K."

"Oh, but there is," T.K. responds, "more good than you'll ever know."

His arm taped securely to his side, he hops off the table, and, leaning heavily on Zack for support, staggers out to the street.

Monday, December 6, 2010

A zealous proponent of the theory that adequate anticipation is the basis of successful manipulation, Pierce Spencer rarely leaves any aspect of his dealings to chance. Every alternative available to him is catalogued, itemized, placed in its proper perspective, chosen or discarded. The survivors are ruminated, modified and polished. When they achieve perfection, when they are clearly incontestable in their infinite superiority, they are doled out to appropriate functionaries, there to be implemented without so much as the slightest alteration.

Today, Spencer has a fair number of such eventualities to untangle, to sort into knot-free fibers, to lay out in fine, straight lines in the bin of accomplishment. The SFL's Divisional Playoffs were held yesterday. Certainly not to Spencer's surprise, the San Francisco Prospectors and the New England Minutemen emerged as winners and will meet in Superbowl XXI on New Year's Day.

Ida Moulay sits across Spencer's desk from him, transcribing his instructions onto a tiny voice-actuated tape recorder.

"I want XXI given saturation promotion," he dictates. "Ten-second teaser spots during station breaks for starters. Get the art department to design a clever XXI logo. Full-page ads in all the general entertainment newsmags, the specialized journals and the horn sheets. Have our agency prepare three sets of comps, one for each of those three market segments, for my approval. Line up pre-game specials for showing by all our affiliates. Make at least one of them a vivifyzation. Those always go over well when they deal with football. Get Enge to do something on his program. Not just this week, every week from here on out. Issue the usual public relations releases. Include quotes from Barin, maybe even get one from the President. I'll leave that to you. And a direct mail piece. I want a mailer to go out to everyone who has punched up at least one replay in the past year. Stress that this is the game of the century. Promise plenty of action, bloodshed, killing, you fill in the words. And a contest. I want a contest. A 'Pick the Superbowl Winner' contest. Run it in two divisions, junior and adult."

He interrupts his conceptualizing to insert a brief explicatory footnote. "Do you get what I'm striving for, here, Ida? I want XXI to be the number one topic from now until January first. I'll hold you personally responsible for seeing that it is." He slips down into his chair, pulls out a lower desk drawer, and props his feet up on it. He draws his finger across his throat and gestures at Ida's recorder.

Ida snaps a toggle, and the recorder shuts off.

"This game is quite important to me, Ida. So much so that I plan to become personally involved in its outcome. I will be Harv Matision's control for this one. I want you to take over the Prospectors' man. Can you handle it?"

"Yes." She's filled in as a programming adjuster on numerous prior occasions. She knows the procedures quite well.

"Within the next two weeks, I want you to memorize all the offensive and defensive signals for both teams. Also both teams' play books. Go through the files. Become familiar with the behavioral patterns of the twenty-six starters. Review the tapes of every game both teams have been involved in this season. You'll only have enough time to skim the highlights, but do so in enough depth to acquaint yourself with obvious nuances, particularly those of Matision and T.K. Mann." Spencer places both feet on the floor, folds his hands in front of him, and brings his clasped forefingers up to touch his chin. "We're promising our viewers that XXI is going to be something extra. It's important to our credibility that we deliver. Is that understood?"

"Perfectly." Ida squirms in her chair. There is one issue Spencer has glossed over. She debates whether or not to bring it up—Spencer does not take kindly to an underling's discovery of a flaw in his logic—and finally decides its long-term implications far overshadow the possibility of a near-term flurry of verbal abuse. "Mr. Spencer, a question?"

He nods.

"About T.K. Mann. Senator Barin was not particularly successful in dealing with him."

"Unfortunately true." Spencer appears to be not at all threatened by it, a good sign.

"Mann is determined to go to the authorities after the Superbowl."

"Yes."

He's so calm, so unruffled, Ida knows full well he has solved the problem, and her anxiety dissolves. "May I ask how you plan to prevent it?"

Spencer grins, actually grins. In all the years she's worked for him, Ida can count on one hand the number of times she's ever seen Pierce Spencer grin. "Quite simple, Ida. Mann won't go to the authorities because, at an appropriate point during XXI, after we've adequately developed the proper degree of suspense, Harv Matision will kill him."

Friday, December 17, 2010

"We have a special feature tonight," reveals Timothy Enge, "in the Pro Prognosticator portion of our show. By linking the IBC sports data bank together with the talents of our studio vivifyzationists, we've put together a projected thirty-minute simulation of Superbowl XXI." He holds up a flimsy blue sheet of paper of the type his viewers have come to associate with the arrival of a late-breaking flash. "It was only finished moments before air time, I haven't even seen it myself. So why don't we take a look at it together and see who the statistics say is going to win the forthcoming big one."

As in a regular football broadcast, tiny wink lights flash on and off in the lower left-hand corner of the screen, indicating both the amount of playing time elapsed and the amount remaining. The realistic quality of the presentation is enough to satisfy any but the most puristic of fans. Granted, the background frequently grows hazy and indistinct, but the startlingly accurate renditions of each of the players more than compensate for it.

At two hours into the first quarter, the Minutemen get the game's first tally.

Early on in the second quarter, the Minutemen score again. Late in that same quarter, Harland Minick is mortally wounded on a short run off center. Shortly thereafter, the Minutemen take possession of the ball, and score again, although not without casualties. Two of their players are red-crossed on the drive to the goal.

The scene shifts forward to the third quarter. Cartoon figures of Harv Matision and T.K. Mann interlock in an epic struggle. T.K. has the ball, Matision has him down on the ground, is on top of him and within a hair of plunging a knife into his throat. T.K. has the knife immobilized with one hand, while he tries to gain a choke hold with the other. Suddenly, Matision jerks free. His arm plunges downward, but he doesn't get a clean hit, his knife merely grazes T.K.'s neck. At the drawing of blood, the referee blows the play dead. T.K. is red-crossed for the remainder of the quarter.

He returns to action at the beginning of the fourth quarter, but in the meantime, the Minutemen have scored again. The two clubs trade the ball back and forth for several hours; then, with less than thirty minutes left to play, comes the game's blockbuster.

T.K. Mann has the ball. He's all alone, within two blocks of the goalyard, and desperately trying to win the Prospectors their first score of the game, when he's collared by Harv Matision. Matision disdains the use of his bola, which would render Mann totally immobile and end the play immediately. Instead, he presses a long knife assault, an action which derives from his penchant for ending a play only by leaving the ball carrier unconscious, bleeding or dead.

In the struggle between them, T.K. does his best to fend off and neutralize his youthful adversary, but he makes too many mistakes, misses too many sure openings, gives Matision too many more in return. Finally, with sixteen minutes left in the game, Matision connects with a perfect straight-in thrust to the base of T.K.'s helmet.

T.K. staggers backwards, yanks his helmet from off of his head, and topples over onto his side, dead, the gold thirteen on the back of his jersey mottled red with his blood.

Harv Matision stands over him, tentatively touches him with his toe, then kicks him once, as hard as he can, in the small of the back.

Fifteen minutes later, the game is over. The Minutemen win it, twenty to nothing.

"Well, that was certainly some prognostication," remarks a stunned Timothy Enge. "Wrapping it up for you, according to our data bank's calculations, the Minutemen will win Superbowl XXI by the astoundingly low score of twenty to nothing, and, in the fourth quarter, Harv Matision will kill T.K. Mann."

Enge takes out the top sheet of paper on his clipboard, studies it for a moment and shakes his head. He wads the paper into a compact ball and drops it to the floor. "What more can I add to a prediction like that except to say, be with us, right here, on New Year's Day, and find out whether or not it comes true."

Monday, December 20, 2010

Contrary to the rosy reports published in various newsmags and sporting journals, participating players detest the four-week layoff between the end of the regular season and the Superbowl. They would be much happier if they could get it over and be done with it. During such a break in their seasonal regimen, their bodies have a chance to mend, but they also have a greater opportunity to become flabby, both physically and mentally. Deprived of the weekly toning rigors of a game, players must turn, instead, to cross-country running, isothenics, weight training, and, even worse, daily practice sessions, all of which they find excessively boring, especially when compared to the exhilaration that accompanies participation in a real game. But the television network requires time to enhance anticipation, boost viewership, so the players wait, wait and train.

The Prospectors' weight room has a solid metal floor covered with six inches of absorbent padding. For their exercises, the players wear special pliant crystalline-flux magnetic belts strapped to their bodies. At prescribed intervals, trainers make the rounds, adjusting the belts to new levels of magnetic attraction, either up or down, depending on a player's particular physical needs.

T.K. is on the incline board doing lung presses. He has twenty pounds of force on each wrist, thirty-five on each forearm, eighty on either bicep, and an additional fifty-five across his chest. This set requires him to do forty-eight repetitions, pause for thirty seconds, and begin again, keeping it up until he has done so eighteen times.

He is midway through when he hears a voice behind him. "Mr. Mann," it says, "Mr. Mann, may I take a moment of your time?" He gazes up into the mirror positioned over his head. There, upside down, looking back at him is Senator Abelman.

"I can't interrupt my workout," huffs T.K.

"Quite all right," says Abelman, coming around to the front of the board so T.K. can see him directly. "What I have to say won't take long. You can listen to me and continue with your exercises both at the same time."

Seeing no way out, T.K. nods.

"I have some information that will, without a doubt, convince you to change your mind, to immediately speak out publicly against IBC." He moves in as close to T.K. as he can get, remaining just outside the radius of T.K.'s pumping arms. "I have heard a rumor," he says conspiratorially, convinced of his new argument's ultimate persuasiveness. "I'll be brutally frank and to the point with you. This rumor suggests that you are to be killed in Superbowl XXI. IBC has it completely arranged."

While T.K. has already guessed as much, to have it confirmed does, nonetheless, upset his concentration momentarily, but only to the extent that he loses count of his repetitions and has to begin his sequence all over. To an observer, the comment doesn't appear to have fazed him in the slightest.

Aghast at T.K.'s apparently callous acceptance of so shocking an assertion, Abelman continues with a good deal less presumption. "This abominable act is to insure you will not have the opportunity to come forth after the game. In light of this, I urge you to reconsider your earlier decision. Come forward now."

Without breaking rhythm, T.K. shakes his head.

Abelman straightens up, shocked disbelief on his face. "I can't even pretend to understand your logic in this matter, Mr. Mann. Your self-centered view of reality. You're not immortal. If they say they're going to kill you, they will." He moves behind the board so he can, using the overhead mirror, look T.K. directly in the face. "Since there seems to be nothing more I can possibly tell you that might influence you, I'll take my leave. Good-by, Mr. Mann. And good luck. I sincerely believe you'll need it."

Shoulders sunken, head bowed, Abelman shambles out the door.

In the overhead mirror, T.K. watches him go, honestly sorry for him, for the ridicule he's undergone, for the sense of utter defeat he must now be feeling. Would that T.K. could tell him how close, how very close he is to achieving his goal. Not before the Superbowl as he wishes, no, but then, not after it, either. During. T.K. plans to do his utmost to see that Senator Abelman has his objectives fulfilled during the Superbowl, on nationwide television, in full color, before what may well turn out to be the largest audience of all time.

The Economics of Superbowl XXI

To a large degree, the entire Superbowl is an IBC subsidization. The network pays team owners, players and sideline patrols directly, and, indirectly, reimburses displacement village operators, officials, street keepers and the whole superstructure of trainers, coaches and statisticians that make up a professional football team. Still, in spite of all this, IBC stands to make an after-tax profit of a billion and a half dollars on the live presentation of this game alone. And IBC will retain full rights to all game tapes for a twenty-year period. Future showings will foster residual income of at least an equal amount. If considered as one lump sum, all the revenue to eventually be generated by Superbowl XXI would be more than enough to place IBC well up on this year's listing of the 500 most profitable companies in the United States.

But all this money is seemingly inconsequential to IBC president Spencer. To him, the phenomenal revenues generated by the Superbowl are purely tangential to the network's real purpose for broadcasting the event. "Television is an entertainment medium," says Spencer. "Football is entertainment. I put the two together the best way I know how. Granted, I make money at it, but that's not my main motivation for doing it. I'm more interested in seeing to it that a lot of fine people take some enjoyment from what I'm doing for them."

If that is his sole criterion for success, he will reach it admirably with Superbowl XXI, when, according to the latest A. C. Neilsen surveys, fully seven eighths of the entire population of the United States will be tuned to his network. (Reprinted from *Business Review,* the issue of Tuesday, December 21, 2010)

Tuesday, December 28, 2010

Feathery quills of sunshine etch stark, angular patterns on the walls in T.K.'s apartment. Even though the glare distracts her from her writing, because sunlight so injects her with the warmth of optimism, Sarah doesn't opaque the windows to blank it out, although, in moments of especially intense concentration, she does tote her vocowriter deep into the cloistered sanctity of a shadow.

She is at just such a point, absorbed in working out a particularly difficult passage, immersed in the intellectual mulch of blackness, when the vid-phone buzzes. Straining to hold to her mental focus, she ignores the vid-phone's braying insistence, hoping the caller will give up and leave her to get on with her cerebral labor, but the vid-phone continues to buzz, until, finally, her contemplation melts away under the heat of her caller's persistence.

She answers the call. It's Coach Carrera. "Oh, Sarah," he says with a strong twinge of disappointment. His voice is muffled at irregular intervals by the sound of airplanes taking off in the background. Clusters of people, many clutching luggage, pass in and out of view behind him. "Is T.K. there by any chance?"

"No," she responds curtly, eager to return to her work. "He left for the airport better than four hours ago. In fact, I thought your flight left right about now." As she sees the concern flood across his face, as the impact of his call slips through to her, all thoughts of her work vanish. She stammers slightly. "Is . . . is there anything wrong?"

Coach Carrerra rubs apprehensively at his cheek, pushing it around in vigorous circles. When he removes his hand, the side of his face is a bright patch of scarlet. "Looks that way. I'm at the airport now. I put the team on the plane. They're gone, but I stayed behind. To track down T.K." Here he holds up a ticket, presumably T.K.'s. "He didn't show up for the flight. He didn't call, he didn't leave any message with anybody, he just didn't show up." Again he digs his hand restlessly into his cheek, kneading his skin, once more, to a burning flush. "Do you have any idea where he might be?"

Sarah considers it. One possibility comes immediately to mind. "This is a long shot, but try the Shaws."

"The who?"

"Frieda and Tanner Shaw. In Dos Palos. They keep T.K.'s—" She halts when it dawns on her that T.K. may not have let his coach in on this aspect of his life. "Give me your number. I'll call them, and buzz you right back."

She punches in the code for the Shaws, fidgets through a twenty-second commercial for Grass Valley cigarettes, and finally gets Tanner Shaw on the screen. "Mr. Shaw," she says, "remember me? Sarah Lauffler?"

"Sure, Miss Lauffler, you came here a while back with T.K. Ain't it a small world, though? I was just asking T.K. how you was."

Just asking him! "Then T.K. is there with you now?"

"Nope. Was, but he ain't now. He took his automobile out for a drive. 'Bout three hours back."

"How soon do you think he'll return?"

Tanner scratches the back of his head. "Funny 'bout that. Only one road down here isolated enough he can drive that machine of his on. 'Bout five miles long, and he gets bored with it after a while, so he tells me, so he don't generally stay out more than half an hour, forty-five minutes, max. But this go-round, he's been out, like I said, for better part of three hours and still no sign of him. I hope he ain't come to no harm."

"So do I, Mr. Shaw. So do I."

She breaks the connection, and punches up the airport number given her by Carrerra. She taps her fingers nervously on the vid-phone controls while the Grass Valley commercial runs its course. Carrerra answers.

"Coach Carrerra, I have a strong hunch I know where T.K. is, but in order to get there, I'll need a helicopter. Can you arrange it?"

It's not an easy request to grant. The environmental laws place equally strict controls on airborne vehicular usage as on ground traffic. Getting a helicopter means special authorizations, permits, justifications, all sprinkled liberally with bribes, not to mention the difficulty involved in scouting up a helicopter with both an adequate supply of fuel and an ample allotment of flight time remaining this late in the month. "You're sure you know where he is?" Carrerra asks, subtly pressing for details of a more reassuring nature.

"Almost positive," she responds succinctly.

It's not exactly the amplification he wanted, nor the encouragement, either, but, everything weighed in the balance, Carrerra decides he has no choice but to go along with her. "I'll call you back."

Sixty minutes later, the vid-phone buzzes. "Be at the airport in half an hour," Carrerra tells her.

The helicopter, a three-seat Bell Python, is a war surplus Army model, still painted its original camouflage colors, brown, green and black, the coloration of the Amazon rain forest. The words U. S. ARMY in black have been amateurishly overpainted with a golden legend, *C. Lukas, Cropdusting*. Large silver canisters have been welded to the helicopter's main frame above its skids. The two-bladed turbo-ended rotor whirls noisily overhead.

Only Sarah and the pilot are in the craft. Naturally, Coach Carrerra wanted to come along, too, but Sarah pointed out that there were only three seats. One of them would be necessary for transporting T.K. and, since she refused to divulge their ultimate destination, she had to go along to give directions. Reluctantly, Carrerra stayed behind.

As the pilot passes over Dos Palos, Sarah gives him his first clue as to his final destination. "Is there an old road of any sort leading from here to Armona?" she asks. He rotates in his seat and gives her a quizzical look. "Yeah, there's old Route Ninety-nine out there. I don't know what kind of shape it's in, though. Ain't been used for years." He sticks his tongue into his cheeks for a spell before he goes on. "Don't let me tell you your business, ma'am, but if you're looking for somebody, you ain't gonna find him between here and Armona. That's all government farmland. First off, they got a fence all the way around it to keep people out. Secondly, must be seventy-five miles to Armona. That's quite a ways to pedal a bike."

She thought it prudent to keep from him the fact they were hunting a man in a car, not on a bike. "Just fly it."

Shrugging, he threads his fingers back into the control sockets. The helicopter tilts over on its side in response. "You're the boss."

They pass over the ten-foot-high barbed-wire fence that marks the boundaries of the government's farmland. In vain, Sarah scans the fence row for signs of a break, but sees none. If T.K. did, as she suspects, take his car through the fence, he did it in such a way as to cover all traces of his action.

Mile after mile of the crazy quilt pattern that is farmland passes beneath, brown dissolving to tan, tan to mottled green. Nowhere on any part of the crumbling slab of highway cutting across it does Sarah see a car. They're barely three miles from the deserted town of Armona, and she's almost ready to concede defeat, when she sees it, gleaming red in the sunlight, half buried in an irrigation ditch, tilted forward at a crazy angle, T.K.'s Porsche.

"There"—she points down to it—"there, come in as close to it as you can."

In a welcome display of taciturnity, the pilot refrains from commenting on the legal implications of their discovery. Expertly, he settles his helicopter in barely ten feet overhead, close enough for Sarah to confirm that T.K. is not still inside.

"O.K., go back up. But not too high. We're looking for a house."

The pilot, his eyesight far keener than hers, spots it first. "Off north," he says, "about five miles."

"Take me there," she commands.

They reach it in less than four minutes, a simple, unpretentious house, turned pocked and decrepit by years of neglect. A dusty green ring of what must have once been grass encircles the house for twenty yards all around. At the ring's edge, T.K. Mann, clad only in a pair of shorts, hunches over a shovel, adding one more to the string of deep holes already trailing off behind him.

"Set it down," she says, pointing, "just on the other side of that tree."

The pilot complies.

"Now go off a few hundred yards. Someplace where you can see me if I wave. I want to be alone with him."

The helicopter takes off in a rich cloud of loam.

Sarah walks toward T.K. He continues with his digging, not even pausing long enough to greet her.

In spite of the brisk chill in the air, his body, shaven bare to protect him from the ravages of adhesive tape, glistens with sweat. A bandage, covering the shoulder wound he incurred in the last game of the season, barely hangs on, flapping with each motion of his arm. His clothes lie in a disheveled heap at the green-brown edge of what once marked the boundaries of his childhood.

She stands beside him, waiting for him to speak the first words between them.

Finally he does. "They told me they'd buried explosives here. I've looked for it everywhere. In and under the house, on the grounds. There's no trace of it." His words are slow, hesitant, as if he examines and evaluates each one, floating limp in the air, before he utters another. "I think they're bluffing." He throws down his shovel, pulls himself to the lip of the hole, and sits there, resting, his feet dangling inside.

Sarah kneels beside him. "You're wrong, T.K., you're, oh, so very wrong." She phrases her message with the harsh overtones of certainty. "It's here all right. Exactly as they said it would be." She tells him this without looking at him. "And they'll detonate it, exactly as they say they will. When you've been around them as long as I have, you learn that they never pretend."

He turns his head sideways to stare at her, dumbfounded. "You're one of them?"

"They can be very accommodating, T.K., very generous."

"Your *EBS* article was nothing but a front?"

"Not really. I am an *EBS* writer. I merely have a—shall we call it a part-time job as well."

"Who do you work for? IBC?"

"Indirectly, through Senator Lako Barin."

T.K. shakes his head. "The accommodating, generous Senator Barin." Significantly, his sarcasm is lost on her. "After his visit, I tried getting permission to have my parents moved. Your good Senator Barin personally gave me a call telling me it would take ninety days to process my request. I don't have ninety days. I have Saturday, January first."

Sarah grasps his shoulder, firmly so he's aware of all she's offering him. "Your memories or your retribution, T.K. You have to decide. Which do you want most?"

Instead of answering, he pulls himself to his feet. Choose between memories and retribution. Considering the eventual ramifications of each, it's not much of a choice, really. In fact, no choice at all. He picks up his clothes. "Get that helicopter over here," he says, balancing himself by holding on to her shoulder with one hand while he slips on his coveralls with the other. The hesitation that characterized his earlier statements is gone, his manner is once more firm, direct. "I've got to catch a plane to Boston."

SUPERBOWL XXI, THE GAME

Saturday, January 1, 2011, 6:30 P.M.

T.K. makes it out onto the playing street just as the whistle sounds, beginning the fourth quarter. Had he not beaten the whistle, he would have been banned from participation in the remainder of the game.

The Minutemen kick off from the west end of Myrtle Street. The ball travels the requisite thirty yards, bounces up against a building, hops twice and spins to rest. Before either of the two receiving Prospectors can field it, Harv Matision falls on it, to T.K.'s great relief. T.K. had only to run downstreet to realize how grossly he had overestimated his remaining endurance. As weak as he is, he'll be lucky to last out an hour of normal play, maybe an hour and a half if he conserves his strength, so he has to get to Matision soon, or, the odds are, he'll never get to him at all.

Matision takes Johnson's center, and cuts diagonally down Anderson to Pinckney.

Doggedly, T.K. shags after.

And there, in the shape of Bumbo Johnson dropping behind to provide interference, he encounters the first, and possibly final, obstacle to his tentative strategy. If Johnson hits him, T.K. has no doubt he'll be out of the game for good. Wisely, he attempts to avoid a contact.

Johnson isn't the considerate type, though. To him, all that matters is that his team is down one man, and he regards T.K. as the easiest way to correct that imbalance. Arms to his chest, elbows out, he plows ahead full speed, straight for T.K.

T.K. does his best to evade him, but, his mobility all but destroyed by his failing stamina and the rigidity of his arm, the best he can do is to forestall the end somewhat by ducking behind a light pole, thereby preventing a head-on collision.

Johnson pulls up short. T.K. edges around the pole, keeping it between him and his attacker. But Johnson is a clever faker. Swinging his whole body right, he cuts left. T.K., deceived, leaves himself completely open to a frontal assault. Ineptly, he fumbles his short club into a pathetic defensive set to counter.

Thankfully, as it turns out he doesn't have to.

Just as Johnson reaches a point barely three feet from T.K., Orval Frazier intervenes, pouncing on Johnson and locking him into a choke hold.

He doesn't hold Johnson for long, though. Johnson breaks the choker, and steps in behind Frazier, pulling Frazier's cast up and around as he goes. Such pain is too much for even Frazier to bear. He goes down, dazed and barely semi-conscious. Johnson winds up for a farewell kick. T.K., taking advantage of Johnson's momentary neglect, catches him with a shoulder block, knocking him forward across Frazier's body. Before Johnson can get up, T.K. drops on him, knees first, left knee on the ground, right one on the top of Johnson's helmet, forcing it backwards. He delivers a quick, short club chop to Johnson's neck.

Johnson gurgles once, and is still.

T.K. rolls off him to rest, gasping, on one hand and two knees.

Zack Rauscher and the Minutemen's mediman rush up and cover the two downed players with red-crossed blankets.

With Frazier and Johnson out of it, that leaves only Gus D'Armato, Matision and T.K.

T.K. lifts himself to his feet and staggers down Pinckney, figuring to try and intercept Matision somewhere before he reaches the goalyard.

But halfway to Joy Street, his head begins to spin. He nearly loses his balance, and remains upright only by grabbing fast to the corner of a nearby building. As best he can, he examines his injured left arm. Blood trickles from out of his cast. There's a trail of it staining the snow behind him, marking his serpentine progress to this point.

Besides a loss of balance, he has chills, as well. He has to sit down someplace warm, and soon.

He breaks open the nearest glass door—it leads into a sporting goods store—and goes inside. Clutching to counters for support, he passes racks of handguns and rifles—ironically a good many of the rifles bear Harv Matision's endorsement—display cases of fishing gear, shelves of ammunition, heading, by the most direct route, to the rear of the store. Once there, it takes him but a moment to find the rest room. He gives his referee the signal, one fist upraised, goes inside and closes the door behind him. His referee and cameraman remain outside. He'll have ten minutes alone before drawing a penalty. He pulls open one of the plastic doors enclosing a toilet, stumbles inside and sits down. Ignoring the red light that pops on every time he does so, he pushes the flush button repeatedly. Again and again, the toilet heats up to incineration levels. Its warmth drifts upward and engulfs him in its pleasant embrace. He keeps it up until the toilet becomes too hot to sit on. He moves into the next stall, and starts the process all over.

Suddenly, the rest room door opens. Beneath the toilet's partition, T.K. sees a pair of blue-clad legs, either Zack Rauscher or Gus D'Armato, the only other Prospectors left.

"T.K., you in here?" It's Gus.

"Yeah, Gus. Right here." T.K. swings the door open so Gus can see him.

"Feeling?" Gus asks tersely, his rifle cradled loosely under his shoulder.

"Fine. Give me a couple more minutes, and I'll be ready to go."

"Wait for you outside." D'Armato turns to leave.

T.K. dives off the toilet seat and hits him in the back of the knees. D'Armato falls to the hard ceramic floor with a loud clatter. Before he can recover, T.K. relieves him of his rifle. Holding it one-handed, he pokes it up under D'Armato's helmet.

"What the hell you doing?" D'Armato's eyes bulge beneath his faceplate.

"Improving my odds, Gus. I'm improving my odds."

"What?"

"How did you know I was in here?"

"Saw you come."

T.K. pushes the rifle in harder. "Wrong. At the beginning of this quarter, you were parked six stories up in that apartment house on Temple. The only way you could have known I was in here was if somebody told you I was in here, told you through a little receiver you've got buried in your head."

"T.K., don't know what you're talking about." He raises his hand solicitously, and, in the same motion, yanks at the rifle. T.K. is one step ahead of him, though. He pulls the rifle back out of reach, then swings it through the air, catching D'Armato's helmet with the barrel. D'Armato's head recoils backwards and bounces off a urinal flush plate. His helmet strap, which he loosened when he came indoors, breaks open, and his helmet falls off, giving T.K. the opportunity to hit him again, this time directly on the side of the head.

Dragging himself upright, T.K. leaves the rest room, D'Armato's rifle in his hand. "Hey, ref," he says to his referee. "My hidden safety had an accident in there. Tripped and fell down. Get my mediman out here to red-cross him." He heads for the street, remembers something and half turns. "Oh, and, ref, I'm declaring myself a hidden safety." As the only combative member of his team left, he may assign himself to any position. He will have to remain at that position for the remainder of the play. He can, if he so desires, change to something else at the start of the next play, assuming, as seems highly unlikely at this point, there is a next play.

He reels out into the street, making straight for the goalyard. Under normal circumstances, he would never expect to make it there ahead of Matision, but the situation in this game is far from normal. IBC has to get rid of him. He's injured, weakened and may collapse at any moment. If he's red-crossed, Matision can't touch him. They have to take him now.

As he suspected, he hasn't gone two blocks toward the goalyard before he hears footsteps crunching in the snowdrifts behind him. He breaks into a jog; the footsteps match his pace precisely. He wheels around. There's no one there. Again he moves. Again the footsteps follow, playing a game with him, a deadly version of hide-and-seek, attempting to wear him down so he'll be that much easier for Matision to handle.

He puts up with Matision's harassment as long as he can. Finally, wheezing heavily, he stops at the entrance to an alleyway, and props himself up against a wall, his head thrown back, his neck exposed, gulping for breath. Within seconds, Matision, in a low crouch, the ball tucked into his gut pocket, appears out from around a corner. His hands paw the air, working hypnotically to draw T.K.'s attention. "It's you and me, old man," he jeers. "I got the ball, you got the rifle. Kill me and you win." Matision is relying entirely on Pierce Spencer's control room conviction that T.K. is too far gone to fire an accurate shot.

T.K. raises his rifle, aims it in Matision's direction and starts to squeeze the trigger, but his arm begins to shake. The twitching spreads with awesome rapidity across his body, until he can hardly stand up. Limply, he slips to the ground, and sits there, his left hand a slimy red, his jaw trembling, his rifle carelessly perched across his lap.

Matision towers over him. "I thought you'd be tougher than this, old man," Spencer instructs him to say for the benefit of the viewers at home. "I guess I gave you credit for more than you're worth."

He reaches down for T.K.'s neck, flexing his hands to loosen them up for the administration of a stranglehold.

He has them almost under T.K.'s helmet when T.K. erupts. He jams his rifle butt up into Matision's Adam's apple. Coughing and gagging, Matision lurches sideways, tugging at his helmet strap, loosening it in a vain bid to draw torrents of cooling air into his injured throat.

T.K. rolls over on his stomach, and pulls himself forward, until he's within two feet of the prone Matision. Then he sticks the end of his rifle up against Matision's head. Because there are just the two of them left (the two medimen not counting), and the last survivor wins regardless of score, T.K. has simply to fire, and he not only gains his revenge, but he wins the Superbowl, besides.

But he does not fire. He has another, larger score to settle, first. Keeping the rifle firmly pressed against Matision's temple, T.K. struggles to his feet. "Get up," he tells Matision.

The two referees, his and Matision's, stand off to one side, exchanging puzzled glances.

"Move," T.K. tells Matision once he's up. "That way." He indicates with his head that he wants Matision to move east down Myrtle.

Completely baffled, T.K.'s referee steps forward. "Mann," he says, "I don't know what it is you think you're doing, but if you don't immobilize that ball carrier and do it soon, I'm going to blow this play dead."

"Stick it up your ass," says T.K., barely getting the words out before the referee blows his whistle.

"That's it, Mann," says the referee. "Play's over."

"Nope," counters T.K., "this play's over when I say it is, and I don't want anybody telling me differently." He moves the rifle a fraction of an inch in his referee's direction, enough so there's no doubt as to his meaning.

Never having encountered such a situation before, the referees have no idea how to deal with it. They do carry pistols to protect themselves in the event an enraged player attacks them, but T.K. is certainly not enraged, at least not at them. Using their radios, they attempt to contact some higher authority for instructions.

Before they can, T.K. marches Matision across to Myrtle, past Hancock and Temple, to Bowdoin.

He waves his rifle side to side, and a wide hole opens in the six-deep line of fans who ring the playing area hoping for a live peek at the action. "Mann, you're out of bounds," yells a member of the Guardsman Sideline Patrol Force when T.K. crosses Bowdoin, but T.K. ignores him. Since his job is to keep people out, not players in, the patrolman doesn't interfere.

A stark, drab gray trailer is parked at the intersection of Ashburton and Somerset. Followed by an ever growing throng of inquisitive spectators, T.K. marches Matision up to its door. As he expected, it's locked.

Holding Matision at bay with the rifle, he bashes at the door with his foot. Control rooms were never meant to protect their inhabitants from ardent assaults, only from curious pryings. T.K.'s kick tears the door from its hinges.

T.K. shoves Matision inside.

T.K.'s eyes take a moment to adjust to the increased light level, but once they do, he sees Timothy Enge, gaping, in a glassed-in booth to the trailer's rear. A white-haired man, most likely the program co-ordinator, his backup behind him, and the two co-head referees stare first at T.K., next at his image projected on several of the screens in front of them. Cameramen relegated to standby duty, having been assigned to players now out of the game, shift their positions nervously, not sure whether to remain at their cameras or duck for cover. To their professional credit, all choose to remain.

In a corner, where they have a view of the entire room, Pierce Spencer and Ida Moulay sit before two high-frequency broadcasting sets. Ever since T.K. made his move and it became apparent to them what he was up to, they have been frantically attempting to stop him, first through the referees, next through the Sideline Patrol Force, finally through the police, but their efforts came always scant minutes too late.

"Everybody against the wall. Everybody but you." T.K. indicates one of the cameramen. "You keep your camera on Matision."

Slowly, reluctantly, the trailer's inhabitants line up against the wall, right below Enge's booth.

"You, PCO, you cut this off the air and you're a dead man. You, cameraman, you come in close on Mr. Matision, here. He's got something he wants to tell all his fans. Something about a little helper he's got buried in his head."

Matision's face contorts with a combination of humiliation and fear. "No, no, I won't."

"Yes, you will," says T.K., and he sticks his rifle into Matision's ear. "Or I'll blow your head open and pick that receiver out of your brains. Either way, they find out. It's just gonna be a lot less messy if you tell them instead of me. Now tell them." He prods Matision hard.

"Yeah, yeah, O.K. I've-got-a-receiver-in-my-head." His confession comes out as a single word.

"Who put it there?"

"He did." He points toward Spencer. "Him and her together." He includes Ida Moulay in his condemnation. "Five years ago. When I was just starting out. They talked me into it. I didn't want to do it, but they talked me into it."

"And how does it work?"

"They feed me information during games. So I can stay on top of the action."

"Does anybody else have one of these?"

Silence.

"Well, do they?" He pokes Matision again.

"Yeah. There's one guy on every team with one. One guy on every team."

"He's lying," shouts out Spencer.

"Oh, is he?" wonders T.K. aloud. He shoves Matision against the wall. "Come over here then." He points his rifle at Spencer. "And give us your version."

This is something Spencer hadn't expected, something he hadn't planned on, drawn up contingency schemes to counter, and, as his precious control slithers inexorably away, so, too, does his backbone. Lumbering meekly, he comes over and stands beside T.K. T.K. puts his rifle against the base of Spencer's neck. "Give us your side of the story." He pushes the rifle upwards. "Is Matision telling the truth?"

Spencer mumbles something.

"Speak up. We can't hear you. Is Matision telling the truth?"

"Yes, God damn you," Spencer bawls. "But there's nothing harmful in it. We're only adding additional interest to the game."

"Yeah," says T.K., "that's swell. I'm sure Eddie Hougart

would have been real happy to hear that." He points with his rifle. "Get over there with the rest."

Spencer joins the others.

"Cameraman, point that thing at Matision," T.K. commands. "I want the folks at home to have a really close-up view of his final performance." He raises his rifle to shoulder level and sights down the barrel at Matision's head.

Matision begins to tremble. "No," he babbles, "no, please." He drops to his knees. "I didn't want to do it. I confessed it just like you wanted me to. Please don't kill me. Please. I don't want to die. I never wanted to die. That's the only reason I ever did it at all. Because I don't want to die."

T.K. squeezes the trigger, slowly applying pressure to it. Then, all at once, he drops the barrel to the floor. The gun goes off, blowing a massive hole six inches in front of Matision. "Matision," says T.K., "I don't have to kill you. Know why?" Matision is crying with loud, wailing sobs. "Because you're already dead. There's nothing inside you with any life left in it."

T.K. ejects his empty shell, throws the gun to the floor, turns and walks out into the brisk chilliness of the night, pushing his way through the hundreds of spectators huddled around the trailer door.

Even as T.K. disappears around a corner, a brawl breaks out in the control room as twelve fans fight for possession of the six-ounce brass casing that was the last bullet fired in Superbowl XXI.

Saturday, January 1, 2011

At the flick of a switch in an IBC office in New York City, an abandoned farmhouse in California erupts out of the ground like blood spurting from a mortal wound, and collapses in around itself. A second and a third explosion reduce it to dust.

You Are the Game of Football

If you paid attention all the way through, you now know as much as I do about street football. There's nothing else I can tell you except for making one last point.

You voted for football, you back it, you make it everything it is today. More so than with any other game ever before, you are the game of football. It's exactly the game you want it to be, hard, fast and lusty.

So do me a favor.

Keep it that way.

You do, and I guarantee you you'll never die of boredom. At least not during football season on any Sunday between 12 A.M. and midnight.

(Herb Carrerra, *Run to Midnight* [Miami: Gridiron Press, 2004], p. 256)

Saturday, January 1, 2011, 9:48 P.M.

"What the hell was that all about?" Eustis Conrad points his beer can in the general direction of the television set. The screen has gone blank. "Where the fuck is the rest of the God-damned football game?"

His wife, Jenine, slaps the set with the palm of her hand. Nothing happens. She slaps it again, and then kicks it, gently once, not so gently again. Still nothing. "Gee, U, I never saw nothing like that before. In all the years I been watching football, I never saw nothing like that. What did T.K. Mann think he was doing? I mean, forcing Harv Matision to leave the street that way, and making him say all those dopey things about him hearing voices in his head. What do you suppose T.K. was trying to prove? He had Matision cold out on the street. Why didn't he shoot him? It would have been such a perfect ending if he'd shot him right off, instead of carrying on the way he did and leaving the whole game up in the air like that. I mean, who won? We got this pool down at the factory, and in order for somebody to get all the money, we first got to find out who won."

"Christ, a man can't even have a simple night of watching football, anymore," grouses Eustis, "without some queer cocksucker coming along and fouling it up. I feel like writing a letter to my son-of-a-bitching congressman, that's how pissed off I am with that faggoty Mann. That son of a bitch. I get one night of relaxation a week, and he has to screw it up. I hope they kick his ass out of football for good for pulling a God-damned stunt like that." He stares around the living room, as if seeing it for the first time. "What the hell are we supposed to do now?"

Jenine shrugs. "I don't know." She too looks blankly around the living room. "Guess I'll go to sleep."

"Shit," groans Eustis. "I suppose that's about it." He chugs his beer, scoops out the last of the peanuts and gets up. "What a fucking heap. Me. Going to sleep at ten-fucking-o'clock on a Sunday night."

Still clinging to the slender hope the TV may yet come back on sometime during the night and either resume the game or allow him to punch up some replays, he leaves the set turned on and dials the volume control all the way over to full. He takes one last, hopeful look at the screen. It's still blank. "Son of a bitch," he says. He doesn't shut the bedroom door.

Bright and early the next morning, for the first time in his life, Eustis Conrad does, indeed, write up and send off a letter to his congressman. Jenine adds a poignant P.S.

APPENDIX

Here's your free personal souvenir program for Superbowl XXI.

Tear it out and keep it near your television set for fast, easy reference during the game.

The Teams

Never before have two Superbowl teams been so radically different.

The San Francisco Prospectors, under the leadership of T.K. Mann, play a slow, conservative, mainly offensive game. They led the league this year in yards gained rushing, but had the league's lowest LPR and KIP. With an average age of twenty-nine (up nearly four years from their average in Superbowl XX), they're the oldest team in the league, a statistic reflected in their relatively lackluster fourth-quarter performances during the regular season.

Experts look for them to attempt to pass their way to an early lead and then try and hold on to it by stalling in the game's later stages.

The main strength of the New England Minutemen, quarterbacked by the sensational Harv Matision, lies in a stunning defense. The Minutemen gave up less ground, and had a higher collective kill ratio than any other team in the league. Only twenty-five years old on the average, they have less experience than the elderly Prospectors, but far more endurance.

Experts expect them to go with a strategy of decimation, killing or wounding as many Prospectors as they have to to insure themselves a victory.

In a hotly fought contest earlier in the year, the Prospectors handed the Minutemen their only loss of the season. The Minutemen are extremely eager to prove, via this return match, that the victory was nothing more than a lucky fluke.

The Pro Grid Line rates the Minutemen a slim seven-point favorite to win, thereby retaining their Superbowl Crown.

Other odds being quoted include 2 to 1 in favor of Harv Mation staying alive, and, in a startling development, 10 to 1 against T.K. Mann doing the same.

TEAM LINEUPS

San Francisco Prospectors

Team Colors—Blue and Gold

No.	Player	Primary Positions Offense/ Defense	College	Age	Ht.	Wt.	Years in SFL
43	Varnie Pfleg	T/L	U.C. Davis	28	6'2"	198	6
21	Buddy Healy	T/L	U. of Illinois	30	6'3"	212	9
25	Ken Dedemus	G/L	Butler	26	6'3"	215	4
18	Lester Brye	G/L	Fullerton State	25	6'	201	2
91	Harland Minick	C/L	Tulsa	26	6'1"	215	3
9	Ros DeGeller	End	Xavier	30	6'9"	232	8
7	Mike Michalski	End	Utah	24	6'10"	248	2
26	Lammy Howe	HB/DS	Temple	29	6'6"	233	7
33	Hellinger Clausen	HB/DS	Colorado	31	6'4"	221	11
12	Orval Frazier	FB/MLB	Grambling	26	6'8"	248	7
86	Gus D'Armato	HS	none	29	6'1"	194	10
1	Zack Rauscher	MM	Michigan	38	5'6"	141	6
13	T. K. Mann	QB/FS	Ohio State	34	6'2"	226	13

New England Minutemen

Team Colors—Red, White and Blue

No.	Player	Primary Positions Offense/ Defense	College	Age	Ht.	Wt.	Years in SFL
12	Bud Barnes	T/L	Arizona State	23	6'3"	212	1
15	Wayne Freedman	T/L	St. John's	24	6'6"	241	2
28	Poco Lambert	G/L	Maryland	21	6'	218	1
35	Hugh Kriller	G/L	TCU	26	6'1"	206	3
16	San Serra	C/L	Bucknell	23	6'3"	221	2
66	Major Parks	End	Willamette	24	6'8"	229	2
72	Wade Heath	End	Stanford	26	6'8"	241	3
24	Howie Underhill	HB/DS	Fresno State	22	6'7"	235	1
39	George Turchen	HB/DS	Ohio State	28	6'9"	250	5
51	Ralph "Bumbo" Johnson	FB/FS	UCLA	26	6'11"	284	5
44	Gunter Schaff	HS	USMA/West Point	30	6'1"	189	10
1	Leo Purvis	MM	Johns Hopkins	34	5'8"	136	6
69	Harv Matision	QB/MLB	none	24	6'5"	218	5

The Playing Area

BOSTON

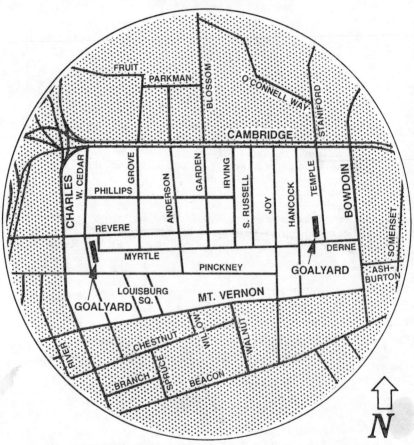

Map 2009. Reproduced courtesy of Philip Bauer Cartographic Projections, Chicago, Illinois.

The playing area for Superbowl XXI was once one of the most prestigious residential locations in Boston. Such well-known people as Hearst Brockington, Louella Gold and Jason B. F. Krull all lived there at one time or another. The area still harbors Boston's Institute of Contemporary Art and portions of Suffolk University.

The entire section is slated to be rebuilt as part of Boston's Model Cities Project, a low-cost housing and urban redevelopment undertaking scheduled for completion in August 2015.

While several brand-new skyscrapers have already been erected in conjunction with the area's modernization, an older form of architecture predominates. Old-style, low-lying brick row houses, shops and office buildings, honeycombed with alleyways and riddled with tiny alcoves, offer countless offensive and defensive opportunities.

Football experts rate the area slightly in favor of the Minutemen with their hard-charging style of play, although most agree that the Prospectors, should they prove able to overcome the strong Minutemen defense, will find the area uniquely well suited to complex offensive strategies, as well.

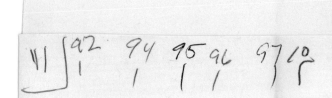

NO RENEWALS!

PLEASE RETURN BOOK AND REQUEST AGAIN.